FALLING FOR THE HIGHLANDER

A Time Travel Romance (Enchanted Falls Trilogy, Book 1)

EMMA PRINCE

Books by Emma Prince

Highland Bodyguards Series:

The Lady's Protector (Book 1)

Heart's Thief (Book 2)

A Warrior's Pledge (Book 3)

Claimed by the Bounty Hunter (Book 4)

A Highland Betrothal (Novella, Book 4.5)

The Promise of a Highlander (Book 5)

The Bastard Laird's Bride (Book 6)

Surrender to the Scot (Book 7)

Her Wild Highlander (Book 8)

Book 9 coming Fall 2018!

The Sinclair Brothers Trilogy:

Highlander's Ransom (Book 1)

Highlander's Redemption (Book 2)

Highlander's Return (Bonus Novella, Book 2.5)

Highlander's Reckoning (Book 3)

Viking Lore Series:

Enthralled (Viking Lore, Book 1)

Shieldmaiden's Revenge (Viking Lore, Book 2)

The Bride Prize (Viking Lore, Book 2.5)

Desire's Hostage (Viking Lore, Book 3)

Thor's Wolf (Viking Lore, Book 3.5)

Other Books:

Wish upon a Winter Solstice (A Highland Holiday Novella)

To Kiss a Governess (A Highland Christmas Novella)

Falling for the Highlander: A Time Travel Romance (Enchanted Falls, Book 1)

FALLING FOR THE HIGHLANDER

Falling for the Highlander: A Time Travel Romance (Enchanted Falls Trilogy, Book 1) Copyright © 2018 by Emma Prince

For Scott. Always.

Chapter One

"Ready?"

Caroline glanced at Hannah, then Allison. Her middle sister's hand firmly clasped hers, but Caroline didn't miss the faint tremble in Hannah's fingers. She gave Hannah's hand a reassuring squeeze, her lips spreading into a smile.

"On the count of three. One... two... three!"

As one, the sisters launched from the mossy rocks and into thin air.

A shriek of excitement tore from Caroline's throat. Her ears filled with the whoosh of air and the roar of the waterfall beside them. Though Leannan Falls was about twenty feet high, the water in the pool below seemed to rush toward her with dizzying speed.

But this was why they'd come to Scotland—for adventure. To make memories that would last a lifetime —together. If practical, type-A Hannah and gentle Allie would've had their way, they would have kept to the path, taken pictures of the falls from a safe and sensible distance. If it hadn't been for Caroline urging them to have some fun, they wouldn't be soaring over the edge of the falls right now.

Or more like plummeting. Caroline's heart leapt into her throat as she stiffened in preparation for contact with the water.

Just then, the pool below seemed to waver, as if it was being shaken out like a spread picnic blanket. Allie and Hannah's hands evaporated from Caroline's. Maybe they'd just let go in anticipation of hitting the water.

Caroline didn't have time to contemplate that further, for a fraction of a second later, she plunged into the pool. Her momentum carried her deep. With the water swallowing her, the whole world went quiet, and all she could hear was her own heartbeat. It thrummed with excitement—and a twinge of unease.

She tried to surge toward the surface. Where were her sisters? Had they felt the same rush she had—and seen the strange shimmer of the water just before they'd broken through?

But before she could emerge from the water, everything began to tilt and whirl. It was like she'd been trapped in a washing machine on full spin cycle.

She opened her mouth to scream, but water rushed in. She felt herself being pulled down—and *through* something that was thicker than water. It tugged at her, stretched her until her skin burned. A blast of light blinded her even though her eyes were closed.

Just as abruptly as it had begun, the spinning

stopped. Her limbs floated in suspension, buoyed by the water's gentle caress.

Water. She was still underwater. Lungs burning, Caroline tried to orient herself. Which way was up? Her mind was already growing hazy from lack of oxygen. She thrashed, wasting precious energy, until she felt herself drifting upward. Kicking and pulling with the last of her strength, she broke free and shot into the air.

Caroline dragged in greedy gulps of air, though it made her sputter and cough. When she'd finally caught her breath, the haze began to ebb from her brain.

But even before she blinked the water from her eyes, Caroline knew something was very wrong.

She couldn't hear the roar of the falls or the slap of water against the pool in which she treaded. Her eyes snapped open, to be met with unfamiliar surroundings.

What the hell…?

She was in a lake. The water was calm except for where it rippled around her. A dozen yards away, a pebbly beach skirted the water, and beyond that was an expanse of lush green grass.

Gone was the waterfall. Gone was the pool she'd jumped into.

And gone were her sisters.

Caroline thrashed toward the shoreline, her stomach twisting with panic.

"Hannah! Allie! Where are you?"

When her bare feet scraped against the rocky lake bottom, she winced. She'd taken off her shoes at the top of the falls before they'd jumped. The gears in her mind lurched and grated to comprehend what the hell had happened since then, but she couldn't freak out and lose it now. Not when she needed to find her sisters.

"Hannah!" she screamed again, fear edging her voice. "Allie!"

Her only answer was silence. She dragged herself onto the lake's shore, her gaze sweeping frantically over her surroundings. The sun was bright and cheery overhead, the vibrant blue sky mottled with puffy white clouds. A gentle breeze made the verdant grasses and the trees beyond sway gently.

The rolling landscape looked much like what she and her sisters had seen over the last two weeks on their vacation. Was she still in Scotland, then?

She pulled in a deep breath, preparing to call for her sisters again. Just then, the ground beneath her hands and knees began to tremble. The tremble turned into a rumble that sent vibrations up her arms and legs.

Caroline's head snapped up. Ahead, a band of men mounted on horseback crested the grassy rise— barreling straight for her.

She scrambled to her feet, but once she was upright, she froze. Should she try to flag the men down? She'd sound completely crazy if she told them she'd jumped into a waterfall and popped up in this lake. Then again, maybe they'd seen her sisters.

That decided it. She waved her arms at the approaching men, but as they drew nearer, her stomach dropped with trepidation.

The men all had on some sort of costume. They wore fitted pants tucked into their boots and plain white shirts, with red and blue checked plaids thrown over one shoulder. Craziest of all, they had long swords belted to their hips.

Well, at least their costumes confirmed that she was still in Scotland. But Caroline doubted these LARPers or historical reenactors or whatever they were would be able to help her.

Unfortunately, they'd already spotted her. One of the men at the front of the group shouted something and wheeled his horse toward her. The others followed after him.

The apparent leader reined in before her, and Caroline froze. He was a handful of years older than she was —maybe around thirty. Wavy brown hair touched his broad, muscular shoulders. Even seated atop his horse, she could tell he was tall and powerfully built. He definitely didn't look like the normal reenactor type.

But what made her barely organized thoughts scatter once again for a heartbeat were his eyes. They glowed amber and cut through her like a knife.

The man's dark eyebrows dropped as his gaze swept slowly over her. He said something in a language that might have been Gaelic, but she didn't understand. She opened her mouth to ask him to speak English, but just then the ground began trembling beneath her bare feet again.

The leader's gaze jerked away, fixing on the hills to Caroline's left. She followed his narrowed stare to find another band of mounted men, these ones with red and green plaids over their shoulders, riding hard toward them.

With a barked word that sounded like a command,

the leader dug his heels into his horse's flanks and reached for his sword hilt. All the men behind him did the same, their swords hissing from their sheaths and their horses surging toward the newly arriving group.

Their *metal* swords. Weren't LARPers supposed to use foam weapons? Caroline stood rooted, her jaw slack as she watched in stunned confusion.

The two groups of men drew closer and closer. If this were some sort of Highland Games event or show put on for a group of tourists, they would pull up. They had to. *Now.*

But instead of drawing back at the last moment, they crashed together in a maelstrom of war cries, horses, and weapons.

A shriek of terror rose in her throat as a full-blown battle erupted. Crimson blood flowed as the men savagely hacked at each other. One man's battle cry turned into an agonized scream as he toppled from his horse.

Time seemed to stretch as she stared in horror, yet the skirmish couldn't have lasted more than a few minutes when suddenly a whistle cut through the air.

The second band of men disengaged, wheeling their horses around and fleeing in the direction they'd come. Two of them hastily threw their fallen compatriot over the back of his horse before spurring after the others.

And just like that, the clash was over. Silence fell, broken only by the distant chirping of a bird and the soft rustle of the grass in the breeze. Yet inside, it was as if a bomb had gone off in Caroline's stomach.

Her legs began to tremble so badly that she thought

she would fall on her face to the pebbly shoreline. Yes, she was in Scotland, but this wasn't where she'd been just moments before—*or when*.

Just then, the leader of the first group of men turned and pinned her with his gaze once more. His face was splattered with mud and blood, yet his eyes burned with an amber intensity that made her mouth go dry.

He wiped his blade across his thigh, then guided it into its sheath, never releasing her from his gaze. He murmured something to his men, then urged his horse into motion once again—right for her.

Whatever he meant to do to her, it couldn't be good. Caroline had no intention of standing there like a stump to find out.

She turned and ran for her life.

Chapter Two

Callum MacMoran frowned at the fleeing lass. What the bloody hell was she doing bathing in the loch that divided MacMoran and MacBean lands? And why was she dashing off toward the trees on the loch's south side nigh naked?

Nay, she wasn't quite naked, but what she wore could hardly be considered clothing. The men's trews she had on were cut off well above her knees, exposing every lithe, creamy inch of her thighs.

And on her torso she wore what could only be described as the top half of a chemise. A very revealing chemise. Her shoulders, arms, and the upper slopes of her breasts were exposed for all the world to see.

Mayhap she'd been wearing those strange undergarments to bathe in, but that made little sense. Everyone within a two-day ride knew that Loch Darraig was no place for lolling about. It was one of the many places along the contested border between MacMoran and MacBean land that had turned dangerous of late.

Or mayhap… A new possibility occurred to him as he watched her bolt away. Mayhap she knew very well the risks of that spot. That would explain the terror that had filled her eyes when he'd approached her, and again when the MacBeans had fled, leaving her alone with a band of MacMorans.

Aye, mayhap she recognized his tartan as that of her clan's enemy. If she was a MacBean, it made perfect sense for her to flee him, the MacMoran Laird.

A seed of an idea took root in Callum's mind. He and his men were lucky not to have sustained any major injuries in this latest skirmish. But he'd lost enough clansmen to know that they were tempting fate with every engagement. Next time they might not be so lucky.

What was more, who knew when the MacConnell Laird would be ready to formalize their clans' alliance? With all hope, it would put an end to the MacBeans' troublemaking once and for all, but until then, Callum was on his own.

But mayhap the bonny MacBean lass currently sprinting away could provide a temporary solution of sorts, a wee bit of leverage to force the MacBean Laird to cease his raids and quarrels over where to draw the border—at least until Callum had the support of the MacConnells to quell him.

"Wait here," he said to his men, then squeezed his heels into his horse's flanks.

"Careful with that wee fish, Laird," Bron called behind him. "She seems a slippery one."

Callum ignored the warrior's teasing comment and the chuckles that rose from his men in response. Instead, he trained his gaze on the lass's back. His horse's hooves devoured the distance between them, and even before she could reach the tree line, he was nigh on top of her.

The steed was trained for warfare, and Callum had ridden a horse even before he could toddle. He maneuvered the animal with ease in a tight arc around the lass to cut off her path to the trees. She scrambled to a halt, panting and staring up at him.

He'd been so distracted by her ridiculously revealing garb earlier that he hadn't absorbed just how bonny her face was, but now he looked his fill.

Brown hair so dark that it was nigh black hung in dripping clumps past her slim shoulders. Her blue eyes were light as shards of ice and wide enough to swallow him whole. The apples of her cheeks were flushed pink from her exertion and her lips were berry-red, a stark contrast to her pale skin.

He gave himself a little shake. Bloody hell, now was not the time to be gaping at a lass—a MacBean, no less.

"What is yer name?" he demanded, infusing his low voice with all the authority of his position as Laird.

She blinked at him.

"I ken ye are a MacBean, for I would recognize one of my own clanswomen," he went on with a frown. "No harm will come to ye, lass, but I would have yer name."

She shook her head slowly, and Callum got the

impression that it was more for herself than him. "What the hell is going on?" she muttered.

In *English*.

If Callum hadn't been as good a rider as he was, he might have fallen off his horse.

What the hell was a bloody Englishwoman doing this far into the Highlands? And on the MacBean border, for that matter.

An ominous sense of foreboding swept over him. Though it was rare for the English to venture so far north into Scotland, it wasn't unheard of—but only if they knew they would be safe from the wrath of the majority of Scots who wouldn't welcome their presence.

If the lass wasn't a MacBean, had she been summoned by them? Would Laird MacBean truly harbor an Englishwoman on his land?

It was possible. Though most in these parts detested the English for all the havoc and suffering they'd caused in their seemingly endless desire to conquer Scotland, the Scots had never been a unified people. Even so deep in the heart of the Highlands, alliances and loyalties could shift with the wind. Callum knew better than most that a man would do almost anything if he thought he acted in his clan's best interest.

"Ye are English, then," he said when he could find his tongue again.

Her eyes went even wider. "Yes. Well, no. That is, I'm American. But you speak English."

Callum's brows lowered. What the hell was he supposed to do with that jumbled response? And what did "American" mean?

"Yer name," he said flatly.

She hesitated, but after a moment, she gave in. "Caroline Sutton."

An English name, spoken in the English tongue. Yet she sounded different than any Englishman he'd ever heard. Mayhap she was French, or Irish, or even Flemish.

He muttered a curse. The fact was, it didn't matter. She was on the MacMoran-MacBean border, and she sure as hell wasn't a MacMoran.

His mind made up, Callum leaned out of his saddle and snaked an arm around her waist. She yelped as he plucked her off the ground and dropped her onto his lap.

"What are you doing?" she snapped, struggling in his hold.

Bloody hell. Bron had been right—she was a slippery one. His arm tightened around her, both to prevent her from sliding off his horse and to keep her still so that she stopped grinding her nigh bare arse against his manhood.

For his efforts, he got a sharp elbow to the gut.

"Hold, woman," he grunted. He drew in a breath to calm his temper. If she truly didn't speak Gaelic, then she hadn't understood when he'd said earlier that no harm would come to her.

"I willnae hurt ye," he said again, this time in English.

"Then why the hell did you grab me?" she shot back.

Good God, the lass had a tongue as sharp as his sword.

He didn't have to explain himself to her, but he found himself answering anyway.

"I'm taking ye with me. Laird MacBean will no doubt be interested in yer safe return, and I plan on exacting a price from him in exchange."

The lass's pale blue eyes filled with dread. "Oh, no. I can't go with you. You don't understand. I'm not supposed to be here. I need to find my sisters, and Leannan Falls, and—"

Ignoring her odd rambling, Callum nudged his horse back toward his waiting men. When they began moving, the lass started thrashing even more. He had to drop the reins and use both hands to keep her from flinging herself to the ground. He wrapped one arm around her torso and clamped the other down on her legs. Luckily, his horse was well trained enough that Callum could guide him with just his knees.

"Be still," he ordered, "else ye'll fall and break yer damn neck."

She only struggled harder.

When he reached his men, Bron wore a wide smile and held a length of rope extended toward him.

"Let me go!" the lass shrieked, bucking under Callum's hold.

His men's grins faded at her words.

"She's English?" Bron asked, stunned.

"Aye," Callum grunted, managing to snatch the rope from Bron's outstretched hand and keep the wriggling lass in front of him in the saddle. "Or close enough. I'm taking her to Kinmuir Castle with us. I believe Laird MacBean might be interested in regaining her—for a price."

And that price would be peace—at least for a short while, until Callum could count on the MacConnells' added strength to bring the MacBeans to heel.

As Callum bound the lass's arms to her sides with the rope, Bron eyed her.

"She's a bonny one. If she does indeed belong to the MacBeans, no doubt someone will want her back most dearly."

Just then, the lass lurched toward Callum, teeth bared. He jerked out of the way just in time to avoid getting bitten and finished tying her so that she was forced into immobility. A few of his men whistled and chuckled at the wee woman's fierce display.

Callum wasn't so easily amused. Aye, the lass— Caroline Sutton—must know she was in enemy hands now. She hadn't admitted to being associated with the MacBeans, but then again, little of what she'd said had made any sense at all. If she *was* allied with the MacBeans, he wouldn't expect her to tell the truth anyway.

Aye, he'd use the lass against Laird MacBean to extract a temporary peace from the bastard. Naught was more important than his clan's safety—not even the fiery hellion in his lap.

The decision made, Callum reined his horse toward Kinmuir Castle and dug in his heels.

Chapter Three

As Caroline jostled and bounced in the saddle before the Scottish warrior who'd bound and kidnapped her, the fight slowly drained out of her.

When she struggled against the ropes pinning her arms to her sides, they chafed her bare skin. But when she remained motionless—or at least as motionless as she could atop a moving horse—the bindings weren't so tight as to hurt her.

With his hands gripping the reins, the Scotsman's arms bracketed her, one forearm brushing her back and the other acting as a corded barrier to keep her from toppling face-first off the horse. His thighs were warm and hard beneath her.

This close, she could see the stubble darkening his square jaw and the specks of dirt and blood on his face and shirt. He smelled of male sweat, leather, and faintly of soap. His unnerving amber eyes remained fixed ahead.

Wolf eyes.

Not that Caroline had ever seen a wolf except at a zoo once, and she certainly hadn't been close enough to look into the animal's eyes. But the way the Scotsman's eyes glowed with intensity made him seem part-wild animal.

Judging from the sun, which was drawing downward with the approach of late afternoon, they were riding northeast. They entered a dense, shaded forest and the air grew markedly colder.

Whether from fright or her wet shorts and tank top, Caroline began to shiver. What was happening? One minute she'd been jumping with her sisters over Leannan Falls, which was only a short drive from Edinburgh, and the next she'd surfaced in some lake in the middle of nowhere.

And now she sat tied up in the lap of some strange warrior…

…*In another time.*

No. She shoved the thought away. It wasn't possible.

Maybe she'd hit her head when she'd jumped into the falls and this was all some sort of weird hallucination. That was more believable than the idea that she'd not only been transported to a different part of Scotland, but to a different time as well.

But the man riding behind her certainly felt real.

Just then, he muttered something under his breath and yanked the length of wool plaid off his shoulder. With a flick of his wrist, he swung it around her, enveloping her in its warmth. In *his* warmth. The heat from his body slowly began to seep into her trembling limbs.

As they rode on, her mind played back the events of the last few hours over and over, looking for an explanation.

Everything had been completely normal until she and her sisters had jumped into the falls. This was supposed to be the last day of their two-week trip to Scotland before they returned back home to Mayport Bay, Maine.

With a day to kill before their flight home, Caroline had asked the owner of the bed and breakfast where they were staying what final sights they might see. He'd recommended Leannan Falls, saying something about a legend surrounding the waters there.

Of course, everywhere they went, people were telling them about legends and faeries and magical stones. The Scottish seemed to take their lore very seriously—or at least they played it up for the tourists.

Allie and Hannah had been game to visit the falls, but when Caroline had come up with the idea that they jump from the top, they'd balked. Though Hannah could take on business school at Yale and start her own event planning company, she didn't like heights. And Allie had nerves of steel as a nurse, but outside the walls of a hospital or clinic, she wasn't exactly the daring type.

Caroline had urged them on, though. "The B&B guy said the waters are supposed to have healing properties," she'd chirped. "Come on. It will be fun."

They'd agreed, so they all kicked off their shoes, set aside their purses, and jumped. And then—

Caroline squeezed her eyes shut. She silently screamed at herself to wake up from this dream, to come back to reality. Sure, it was all well and good to *imagine* being kidnapped by some strapping Scottish warrior with piercing honey-colored eyes, but this felt too real. It was time to snap out of it.

But when she opened her eyes again, she was still surrounded by woods, riding atop a horse, sitting in the lap of a strange man.

The trees around them began to thin, and soon they broke onto a verdant expanse of rolling hills. When Caroline's gaze landed on one of the peaks ahead, her breath snagged in her throat.

A stone castle stood in the distance. But it was unlike anything she'd ever seen.

Over the last two weeks, she and her sisters had visited plenty of castles—or rather, *ruins* of castles. The few that were still whole had been built more recently, or at least drastically restored.

This one, on the other hand, was built in the style of the oldest structures they'd visited, except instead of crumbling walls and moss-covered stone, the castle stood whole and solid atop the grassy hill.

Caroline swallowed. "That is…"

"Kinmuir Castle. My home."

She jumped at the man's deep, reverberating reply. They had ridden in silence thus far, but now that she'd broken it, she wanted some answers.

"And you are?"

His gaze met hers, and a strange shiver pricked her skin despite the warmth of the wool plaid encasing her.

"Laird Callum MacMoran."

Laird? Although Caroline hadn't been as interested in all the history and lineage stuff as her sisters on this trip, even she knew that meant he was the head of his clan.

This was all too much to believe.

She narrowed her eyes at him. "Is this some sort of prank? Did my sisters put you up to this? Someone's about to jump out with a camera and yell 'gotcha,' right?"

He frowned at her. "I dinnae ken what ye are talking about. If yer aim is to feign madness to avoid being sent back to the MacBeans, it willnae work."

Caroline opened her mouth to reply, but before she could speak, he said, "Hold yer wheesht, woman. It has been a long enough day as it is."

She bristled at his tone—what the hell was a wheesht?—but it *had* been quite the day already. Her gaze darted back to the castle as they began climbing the rise.

A massive, square stone wall loomed over them, a round three-storey watchtower in each of the four corners. In the middle of the wall rose twin rectangular stone towers that both stood four or five storeys high.

As they drew higher up the hillside, she made out a cluster of thatch-roofed buildings on the far side of the castle—a village of some sort. She didn't have time to see more, for they halted in front of a wide wooden gate set into the wall, a banded metal portcullis lowered in front of it.

Above them, a head appeared over the edge of the

wall. Callum said something in that language she assumed was Gaelic to the man, and a heartbeat later the portcullis began to rise with a groan. When the portcullis had fully lifted, the gates behind it swung wide with a faint squeak.

They rode through the wall and into an open court-yard that bustled with activity. People dressed in plain woolen clothes and red and blue checked plaids streamed toward them, smiling and cheering for the returning men.

A slim-built man with graying brown hair and matching tidy beard approached and said something to Callum. But then the man's eyes locked on Caroline and he froze, his lips parted in shock.

Before he could regain his wits, a short, round woman with wild red hair came bustling up behind him. She, too, began speaking, but Callum cut her off.

"Speak English around the lass," he said flatly. "She doesnae understand Gaelic."

All those gathered in the courtyard abruptly fell silent. The red-haired woman's eyes practically bulged out of her head as she stared at Caroline. Murmurs began rising around them, and a few people pointed at her.

Normally Caroline wasn't one to be embarrassed by other people's judgments of her, but she was just as confused and stunned as everyone else, so she remained silent, staring back at them wide-eyed.

Ignoring the others, Callum shifted beneath her so that he could dismount, then lifted her down from the horse. Instead of setting her on her feet, though, he held her against his chest and strode toward the two rectangular towers, which were connected at their base.

The man who'd spoken before hurried after them, hissing something in Gaelic.

"English, Eagan," Callum snapped, cutting him off.

The man, Eagan, swallowed and began again. "What is an Englishwoman—wrapped in MacMoran clan colors, no less—doing here, Laird?"

"At Kinmuir? I thought it was obvious I brought her here," Callum replied dryly. "I found her by Loch Darraig. And before ye ask what she was doing there, I dinnae ken, but I intend to find out."

As Eagan sputtered in confusion, Callum pushed open the wooden double doors and strode inside, speaking over his shoulder. "Go to my solar and prepare a missive for Laird MacBean. I'll be there shortly."

With a flustered blink and a dip of his gray-brown head, Eagan hurried toward a spiral staircase on the left side of the room they'd just entered.

Or rather, banquet hall. The space was enormous, with high-raftered ceilings making it feel even bigger. Wooden tables and benches were pushed against the walls, except for one large table, which sat atop a raised platform on the back wall. Two hearths that were big enough for Caroline to walk into without bending over sat opposite each other on either end of the space.

As Callum continued toward another spiral stone staircase to the right, Caroline belatedly realized everything in the giant room was mirrored. Two hearths. Two flights of stairs leading to the two towers. And one table in the middle that must be for the Laird.

"Tilly!" Callum bellowed, making Caroline jump in his embrace and cutting off her thoughts.

The red-haired woman came scurrying in through the doors behind them. "A-aye, Laird?"

"I need ye to open the east tower's uppermost chamber."

"But Laird—"

Callum ignored her and mounted the stairs, carrying Caroline higher and higher past several landings until the stairs simply ended in front of one last door. Below them, Caroline could hear Tilly huffing her way upward. When she reached them at last, her face was red and her hair was somehow even frizzier.

She fumbled with a ring of big metal keys dangling from her waist until she found the one she was looking for and jammed it into the lock. It turned with a rusty thunk and the door swung open with a whoosh of cool, musty air.

Callum stepped into the dim room and moved toward a bed on the far wall. Foreboding suddenly flooded Caroline's stomach. She was bound and completely at his mercy, in his castle, surrounded by people who did his bidding.

With the last of her strength, she bucked and tried to break free of his hold. His hands tightened around her for a moment, but then he set her on the bed and stepped back.

"I told ye no harm would come to ye while ye are in my care, and I dinnae ever break my word," he said gruffly.

Caroline sat up and tried to scoot away across the

bed, but the plaid fell from her shoulders and got tangled in her legs.

Behind Callum, Tilly gasped. Caroline turned to find the older woman gazing in horror at the ropes lashing Caroline's arms to her sides.

"Heaven help ye, Laird, what have ye done?"

Tilly hurried to the bedside but halted under Callum's scowl. "I found her on the MacBean border. An Englishwoman."

"So ye trussed her up like a stuck pig?" Tilly demanded.

"The lass attempted to escape and would have killed herself—or both of us—by thrashing atop my horse. And she tried to bite me."

"All the same," Tilly scolded, "is this how ye'd have the MacBean Laird treat one of our clanswomen if she fell into his hands? What if the lass were yer dear sister Thora?"

Callum stiffened at that, his eyes narrowing on the woman. "That is why ye are here—to see to the lass's treatment. Bring her dry clothes and something warm to eat. And light a fire in the brazier—the air is too cold and damp in here."

That seemed to smooth Tilly's feathers somewhat. "Aye, Laird, right away." She hustled on short legs back to the door and disappeared down the winding stairs.

Caroline suddenly became acutely aware of the fact that she was alone with the imposing Scotsman. He turned to her, his amber eyes sharp and unreadable.

He reached for her and she flinched back, but all he did was unfasten the rope and begin unwinding it from her. When she was free, his gaze flickered over her wet clothes. Abruptly, he turned away and strode toward the metal brazier in the corner. While he fiddled with the unlit fire already laid there, she took in her surroundings.

Besides the bed and the brazier, the only other piece of furniture was a massive wooden chest pushed against one wall. A single shutter blocked the only window. That was all.

It seemed she was more prisoner than honored guest in this bizarre hallucination. She almost snorted with mirth at the absurdity of it all.

Callum straightened from the brazier and turned, his mouth opening to say something. But just then, Tilly came huffing and puffing into the room once more, a bundle of folded wool in her hands.

"Here we are, lass," she said, approaching. "These are the Laird's sister Thora's old things, but I believe they'll fit. I set Margaret to work heating some stew, and one of the lads will be up shortly to light the fire."

"I'll be in my solar if ye need aught of me, Tilly," Callum said abruptly, striding toward the door. "Ye neednae linger in here. And Tilly—lock the door behind ye when ye leave."

With that, he disappeared down the stairs. Somehow the bare stone room felt even colder and lonelier now that Callum was gone, even though Tilly still stood before her.

"Well now," Tilly said, forcibly reaching for an air of calm. She extended the stack of folded clothes toward Caroline, who stood from the bed to accept them.

Dread lacing her gut, she set the clothes on the bed and lifted one garment at a time for inspection.

The first was a wool dress dyed blue. The next was like a nightgown made of linen. Below that was a pair of woolen stockings and soft slippers.

Unless she'd stumbled into some weird cult, she had a sinking suspicion about what these clothes meant.

"I'll be back with the stew shortly, Mistress...?" Tilly said, drawing Caroline's attention.

"Caroline," she said. "Just Caroline."

"Verra well, Mistress Caroline," Tilly replied, blatantly ignoring Caroline's weak attempt to avoid a title. "Once ye have a hot meal in yer belly and a fire to cut the chill in here, ye'll feel right as rain, I assure ye."

Caroline very much doubted that. She continued to stare at the pile of clothes on the bed, her mind working to find any other way to explain what was happening.

Just as she heard the door creak with Tilly's departure, her head snapped up. Of course. Why hadn't she thought to ask earlier?

"Tilly?"

"Aye, mistress?"

Caroline dragged in a breath, willing the words out. "What year is it?"

The woman's hazel eyes widened slightly. "Why, it is the year of our good Lord 1394."

Caroline's knees buckled. If it hadn't been for the bed next to her, she would have crumpled to the floor. Distantly, she heard Tilly ask if all was well, but when Caroline didn't respond, she clucked her tongue and quietly closed the door behind her.

The click of the lock sounded over the rush of blood in Caroline's ears.

Oh my God.

This was so much worse than a dream or hallucination. This was a nightmare.

Chapter Four

"**A** missive for ye, Laird."

Callum took the folded parchment from Eagan, instantly recognizing the MacBean seal on the red wax holding it closed.

"Thank ye," he replied with a wave of one hand, effectively dismissing Eagan while keeping his attention fixed on the missive.

Laird Girolt MacBean certainly hadn't wasted any time. It had only been yestereve that Callum had sent a note obliquely referencing an important matter that the recalcitrant Laird might be interested in resolving, and here was his reply this morning.

When the solar door thudded closed behind Eagan, Callum broke the seal and quickly scanned the missive.

To his satisfaction, MacBean had tersely agreed to meet Callum at Loch Darraig the following day to discuss the matter he'd alluded to, yet the man made no mention of Caroline Sutton. Surely if MacBean knew

Callum had the strange English lass in his possession, he would have promised to give the MacMorans hell for taking her, or at least threatened Callum if he dared mistreat her.

Mayhap the lass's disappearance from MacBean land had gone unnoticed thus far, but Callum found that hard to believe. Such a bonny woman could never go unnoticed.

Annoyed with the direction of his thoughts, Callum crumpled the terse missive and tossed it into the fire crackling in the solar's hearth. Though Caroline had been kept under lock and key all night in the highest chamber in the east tower, her presence had hung like a thick Highland fog around Callum last evening and through the night.

He should have been able to set the matter aside after he'd sent the missive to Laird MacBean, but his mind kept returning to the odd lass. After several fitful hours of attempted sleep, Callum had given up and risen, retreating to his solar to escape further distraction.

Instead, he'd spent much of the morning pacing and chewing on her puzzling accent, strange comments, and outlandish garb. Thank God he would be rid of the woman tomorrow—assuming Laird MacBean agreed to a temporary truce in exchange for the lass's return. Then his thoughts would be his own once more.

It seemed that until then, however, he would be plagued by visions of Caroline's startlingly blue eyes, memories of her sharp tongue, and an image of her nigh bare body branded on his mind.

With a muttered curse, he spun on his heels and

abandoned the solar. Without knowing where he was headed, he tromped down the west tower stairs. When he stepped into the great hall, his gaze landed on Tilly, who was backing out through the door that led to the kitchens, a tray laden with food in her arms.

"Ah, Laird," Tilly said, glancing up at him. "I was just on my way to Mistress Caroline. I ken ye wish to see to yer…*guest's* comfort, so I thought I'd bring the lass a wee bite to break her fast before the rest of the castle rises."

It seemed fate was taking pleasure in toying with him, for here was yet another reminder of the woman he was trying so hard to banish from his thoughts.

He let a breath go. Mayhap instead of fighting it, he ought to face that which was so thoroughly preoccupying him. He had quite a few questions about Caroline's origins and appearance on his border—questions Laird MacBean was unlikely to answer. Aye, at least this way he had a legitimate excuse to see her again.

"Allow me," he said, striding toward Tilly and lifting the tray from her hold.

There was naught "wee" about the meal Tilly had assembled for Caroline. The tray was loaded with a bowl of porridge, a pitcher of fresh milk, a half a loaf of bread slathered with butter, a wedge of white cheese, several early-season apples from the orchard, and a pot of honey. Tilly took pride in feeding all those in the castle well, but the lass wasn't some strapping Highland warrior.

Seeming to sense Callum's skepticism over the quantity of food, Tilly folded her arms across her ample chest. "The lass went through quite an ordeal yesterday, to hear Bron and the others speak of the skirmish and how ye found and caught her. She needs to keep her strength up. Besides, that chamber is drafty and the walls are damp and cool even in July."

That was true enough, but even if it wasn't, Callum had learned from an early age not to challenge the stubborn cook. "My thanks, Tilly, for all yer care. Now, yer keyring, if ye please."

With a grumbled comment about bull-headed Lairds, she unhooked the keyring from her belt and handed it to him while he balanced the tray in one hand.

Callum left Tilly behind as he strode toward the east tower stairs. As he began climbing, anticipation coiled in his stomach. With a change of clothes, a night of sleep, and another meal, he hoped Caroline Sutton would be willing to explain things a bit more clearly.

When he reached her chamber door, he didn't bother knocking. Instead, he poised the tray on one hand again and shoved the key into the lock, turning it and pushing the door open in one motion.

"Tilly, how the hell am I supposed to do this? And I don't have any clean underwear. What am I supposed to do, wear nothing under this stupid dress?"

The tray nearly went tumbling from Callum's hand. Caroline stood with her back to him, fumbling with the ties that ran down the back of her gown. With the laces wide open, he got a full view of her chemise, as well as the sloping upper curve of her backside underneath.

"It's no' Tilly," he managed to grind out.

Caroline whirled, her wide blue eyes fixing on him. Callum's mouth went dry. This side of her was even worse. The gown's blue wool hung off her shoulders and sagged in the front, leaving the creamy tops of her breasts on full display above the chemise.

Though he'd seen more of her skin when she'd been wearing those strange undergarments yesterday, this somehow felt far more intimate. They were in a bedchamber. Alone. And she stood before him with her dress nigh falling off.

"Oh!" Judging by the flush creeping from her chest to her cheeks, she too sensed the intimacy of the moment. She snatched her hands from behind her back and clamped them onto the gown's bodice to keep it from slipping further. "What are you doing here?"

He tilted his head toward the tray. "Ye ought to eat," he said brusquely. Clearing his throat, he added, "And I have a few questions for ye."

When she swallowed and nodded, he closed the door and set the tray on the edge of the bed before turning back to her.

"What do you want to know?" she asked warily, tugging up the shoulders of her gown.

Callum muttered a curse. He wouldn't be able to think straight if she continued to stand there half-dressed.

"Turn around," he ordered, his voice coming out gruffer than he'd intended.

She shot him a guarded look, so he added, "I'll no' fetch Tilly away from her duties this morn to untangle the mess ye made of yer laces, so unless ye think ye can do it yerself…?"

Reluctantly, she gave him her back. She hooked a hand around her dark hair and scooped it over one shoulder. Callum had to grit his teeth against the sight of her milky, slim neck. He focused on the knotted ties to avoid staring at the faint blush at her nape, yet his hands still shook slightly as he began untangling them.

To distract himself, he cleared his throat again and spoke. "How did ye get here? To the MacBean-MacMoran border, that is."

"I don't really know where *here* is." She glanced over her shoulder, and his fingers slipped on one of the laces. "Tilly said the year is 1394."

He frowned, not following the lass's abrupt pivot. "Aye, it is."

Caroline closed her eyes for a long moment, then dropped her head. "Somehow this is real," she muttered. "This is happening."

Damn. She wasn't making sense again, just like yesterday. "Ye dinnae remember how ye got here?" he tried again, at last freeing the ties from their knot. He tugged on the laces to cinch up the bodice of the gown, revealing her form underneath. She was slim, but her delicate curves were more than enough to fill a man's hands.

Not mine, he told himself firmly as he worked the ties tighter.

"The last thing I remember was jumping off Leannan Falls."

At last, she'd said something coherent. "I've heard of those falls," he commented.

Her head snapped up and she pinned him with another gaze over one shoulder. "You have?"

"Aye—well, only that they exist. They are past Edinburgh, near the border, aye?"

"Yes," she breathed. "Are we close, then?"

His hands stilled as he tied off the laces. Mayhap he'd been mistaken about her beginning to make sense. "Nay, lass. We are in the Highlands. Edinburgh is nigh a sennight's ride from here."

"A sennight—a week," she murmured. "What the hell happened?"

"Why dinnae ye tell me?" Callum stepped back and crossed his arms over his chest. Whether it was Caroline's nearness or her strange answers to even his simplest questions, he found his thoughts muddled—and his patience wearing thin.

Seemingly in a daze, Caroline drifted toward the bed and sank down next to the tray of food. She absently picked at the bread, opening and closing her mouth several times as if to speak, but no words came. Finally, she lifted her head, and when her eyes met his, they were full of resignation.

"I'm from the future."

Callum blinked. "What?"

"I'm from the twenty-first century. From a country called America. I was visiting Scotland with my sisters for a vacation. I guess you probably don't know what a vacation is," she muttered. "Anyway, on the last day of our two-week trip, we went to Leannan Falls. I talked everyone into jumping off the top. When we did, my sisters vanished and I popped up in that lake—"

"Loch Darraig," Callum interjected, speaking slowly.

"Sure," she replied. "There was a lot of spinning and bright lights, but suddenly I was just…there. And then you showed up, and there was that battle, and now here I am."

Bloody hell. It was worse than Callum had initially thought. Aye, the lass had been cagey before, and down-right odd at times, but he'd assumed it was because she knew she was in enemy hands. He hadn't suspected that she'd fully lost her wits.

"Does this happen to ye often, lass?" Callum asked, trying to keep his voice level. "Falling back through time and waking up in a new place?"

Her lips tightened. "I'm not making this up."

"Och, I ken ye believe what ye're saying. But mayhap that's the problem."

She jerked to her feet then, squaring off with Callum despite the fact that he stood head and shoulders over her.

"I'm not crazy. I'm not lying. And I'm not confused." Her dark brows pinched together. "Well, I'm confused as hell, actually, but I'm telling the truth. I don't know what happened, but whatever it was, I need to figure out how to undo it."

Callum laid gentle but firm hands on her shoulders and guided her back to the bed. "What ye need is to rest yer mind, lass. Try to eat a wee bit. Mayhap sleep some more."

"No," she snapped, squirming out of his hold. "I need to go back to that lake—Loch Darraig—and see if I can reverse whatever happened to me." She began pacing in front of him, her skirts swishing against his leg every time she passed. "Maybe if I jump into the waters, I'll be sucked back to Leannan Falls—and the present. Like some sort of portal or vortex or something."

He had no idea what she was talking about, but it seemed the words were meant more for herself than him. She stopped abruptly, fixing him with her piercing blue gaze.

"Take me back to Loch Darraig."

"Nay," he said without hesitation. The last thing he needed was an addle-witted Englishwoman wandering his lands. And he sure as hell wasn't going to give up his leverage over Laird MacBean.

Guilt pinched his stomach to use her as a hostage of sorts now, seeing as how she wasn't in her right mind. Yet the safety of his clan outweighed his concerns for one lass.

When her mouth fell open at his blunt denial, he added, "Ye are staying here until tomorrow morn, when I'm taking ye back to Laird MacBean. Ye are safe here until then, but ye'll remain in this chamber."

"I'm a prisoner, then?" she bit out.

"Call it what ye like, but ye arenae leaving."

"You don't understand." Her voice was suddenly low and pinched, and her eyes grew damp. "My sisters are probably in the present right now, thinking I'm missing —or dead. I can't leave them—not after what happened to our parents." Her throat closed on the last word, making it little more than a croak.

Caroline swallowed, blinking away the tears, and tried again. "Look. It's obvious I don't belong here. I probably talk funny to you. And I doubt you come across many people in shorts and a tank top around here."

She waved a hand toward the trunk against the wall, where she'd spread out the strange garments she'd been wearing yesterday. Perhaps that was what she'd meant when she'd said she needed more "underwear" earlier.

Callum's gaze landed on a small scrap of soft pink fabric, and a matching object that appeared to be a series of straps attached to two rounded cups just about the same size as Caroline's—

He coughed, ripping his eyes away from the pile of preposterous garments. "Aye, ye dinnae belong here on MacMoran land. But if ye mean aught to the MacBean, come tomorrow ye'll be his problem, no' mine."

Callum turned to leave, his thoughts about this strange lass more muddled than when he'd arrived, but Caroline caught his arm.

"*Please,*" she said. Her hand felt like a small brand on his forearm. Awareness shot through him at the contact, and he sensed his resolve cracking.

Gritting his teeth against the desire to touch her in return, he willed his voice to be even. "I dinnae ken what happened to yer parents, lass, or where yer sisters are, but we are at war with the MacBeans. The MacMoran clan is my responsibility as Laird. I'll have peace from Girolt MacBean in exchange for ye, and that is the end of it."

He turned away and strode out the door. But even after he closed and locked it behind him, the image of her standing rooted with shock, her blue eyes wide and her lips parted, would not leave him.

Chapter Five

"Quit yer squirming, else I'll bind ye again."

Caroline shot Callum a glare. She was tempted to shift in his lap again just to annoy him, but she knew from experience that he wasn't afraid to make good on that promise.

Earlier that morning, he'd fetched her from her chamber-prison and guided her by the elbow out of the tower. For a single heartbeat, hope had surged through her. It was the first time she'd been allowed to leave her room in the two days since she'd arrived.

But when he continued through the tower doors and into the courtyard, where a dozen men on horseback waited for them, her hope died. Of course. He was taking her to Laird MacBean to use as a bargaining chip.

He'd mounted a gray horse and pulled her up across his lap, as he had when he'd first caught her. Then he'd given a whistle, which was apparently the signal to the gathered men to ride out through the open gates.

Caroline had never been comfortable around horses. She preferred to move under her own power, at her own speed. That was why she'd never finished a degree at the University of Maine in Portland—she'd much rather spend a weekend hiking along the Appalachian Trail or slipping off to climb Mt. Katahdin than stay at home studying.

But the truth was, her awkward wriggling in Callum's lap was only partly because she didn't like being atop a horse. His rock-hard thighs under her bottom and his looming presence behind her were…unnerving.

Callum wasn't like any man she'd met in her own time. For someone only a handful of years older than her, he was so confident and capable, so sure in his every motion and glance. That was probably because of his responsibility as Laird.

Of course he was also blunt, stubborn, and over-bearing as well, but he didn't scare her. Not truly. Despite his wolfish glares and brusque commands, he'd kept his word and hadn't harmed her.

And although she tried not to let herself notice, he was undeniably gorgeous. He was all hard lines and sinuous strength, from his chiseled jaw to the wall of his chest and the powerful thighs beneath her. She felt itchy and warm at every point where their bodies touched.

Or maybe that's just this damn wool dress, she thought sourly.

Why the hell were her thoughts betraying her like this? Yes, Callum was attractive. He was tall, broad-shouldered, and corded with lean muscle. This morning, his eyes were the color of liquid honey and he'd bound his chestnut hair at the base of his neck with a piece of leather. He hadn't bothered to shave the dark stubble dusting his strong jawline, but he'd obviously bathed, for he smelled of soap and clean linen and faintly of smoke and leather.

Caroline realized she was staring at him. She ripped her gaze away and shifted in his lap yet again. He responded with a low growl of warning.

What was wrong with her? She should have been plotting an escape now that she was out of the castle, not ogling her captor.

The problem was, she hadn't been paying as close attention to her surroundings as she should have thanks to Callum's discombobulating nearness. Shameful, considering that she'd thought herself something of a tree-hugging outdoorswoman back home in Maine.

Caroline scanned the surrounding woods. They were riding roughly southwest judging from the weak sunlight fighting through the clouds overhead. She'd learned over the course of this two-week trip that even in July, Scotland's weather was fickle.

She wasn't exactly sure where in the Highlands she was, but when she'd passed through earlier with her sisters, she'd identified quite a few familiar plants. Thank God her year as a botany major, followed by another year in the sustainable agriculture program at UMaine, hadn't been a complete waste.

Yet she doubted that she'd be able to survive on wild blackberries and acorns for very long if she tried to make a break for it now. And she had no tools, no gear, nothing but the blue wool dress Tilly had given her and the plaid Callum had slung around her shoulders against the damp, cool morning air.

Besides, she was fairly confident that even if she somehow managed to wriggle off Callum's lap and bolt into the woods, he'd be upon her like a hawk on a mouse, just as he had been two days ago.

No, she was stuck with Callum on this damn horse —well, at least until he turned her over to Laird MacBean.

"So, what's the deal with you and Laird MacBean, anyway?" she asked testily, breaking the heavy silence hanging around them.

Callum gave her a frown. "We dinnae have a deal—*yet*."

"No, I mean…" She searched for the right words. "Why do you need to use me to bargain with him? And why were you and those other men fighting?"

The scowl on Callum's face turned hard with anger. "Ever since I became Laird three years past, MacBean has been challenging me, encroaching on our border to see what he can get away with. It started with a few stolen sheep and cattle, but lately his men have been stealing crops and even attacking MacMoran farmers. We force them back whenever we can, but even spilling their blood doesnae seem to stop them."

Callum huffed a breath as if to release some of his rising ire. "He can have ye back in exchange for his word that he will cease reiving my lands—at least until my alliance with the MacConnells, the clan that borders us both to the south, can be solidified."

Caroline opened her mouth to respond, but hesitated. Though she didn't like the idea of being traded to some other Laird, she had to admit that Callum's motivations seemed honorable enough. In using her, he was trying to protect his people.

All the same, being a pawn between two warring medieval clans wasn't exactly her idea of a good time—not when she needed to find a way back to the present. And her sisters.

Just then, the trees fell away and they rode out onto an expanse of rolling moorlands. In the distance, a ray of sun sliced through the clouds and glinted off a still body of water. Familiarity tugged at her.

"Is that…"

"Loch Darraig." Callum's deep, sure voice reverberating through her shoulder made her jump.

Caroline turned to gape at him. "Why didn't you tell me we were coming back here? I need to—"

Ignoring her, Callum whistled, and suddenly the horse beneath them surged forward into a gallop along with the others. Caroline's words turned into a shriek, and she had to fling her arms around Callum's solid middle to keep her seat.

By the time he reined in his horse along the loch's shore, she felt as though her brains had been put in a blender and her bottom had been paddled black and blue by the jarring sprint.

Loosening her hold around his torso, she touched

shaky fingers to her face to make sure all her teeth hadn't rattled from her head. But when her gaze fell on the calm loch waters once again, all thoughts of the wild gallop fled.

"Let me down. I need to get into the loch. It might take me back to my time."

Callum leveled her with a sharp look, his eyes seeming to glow. "We arenae here to indulge yer madness, lass." His gaze flickered over her head. "Mac-Beans," he said, and the warriors around them instantly tensed. "Keep yer wits, men, and be ready, but dinnae make a move unless I give the order."

Caroline followed the path of his eyes and found a band of a dozen or so mounted men in red and green plaid cresting the nearest grassy rise. It was much the same as it had been two days past—except this time Caroline was right in the middle of things instead of standing on the loch's shore watching. At least no swords had been drawn—yet.

When the group was only a dozen feet away, the man at the front held up a fist and the mounted warriors behind him halted. The man, clearly the leader, appeared to be middle-aged. His black hair was heavily streaked with gray, though his eyes shone with a dark intensity that nearly made Caroline shrink back.

"Laird MacBean," Callum said behind her, his voice guarded.

"MacMoran," the sharp-eyed man replied.

"Let us proceed in English, if ye please, Laird," Callum said.

MacBean's eyes widened a fraction, then flicked to

Caroline. Again, she had to resist the urge to flinch back. This was the man Callum was going to turn her over to?

"Verra well," the Laird replied at last, though his eyes remained narrowed with suspicion. "Ye ken my son, Terek."

For the first time, Caroline noticed a younger man just slightly behind the Laird. He appeared closer in age with Caroline than Callum—maybe twenty-four or twenty-five—but the family resemblance to Laird MacBean was undeniable. Though Terek did not yet bear his father's barrel chest or stocky middle, he had the same dark, keen eyes and black hair.

Terek and Callum exchanged terse, silent nods before Callum shifted his attention back to Laird MacBean.

"I dinnae take kindly to being beckoned to our border without an explanation, MacMoran," the Laird said, glaring at Callum. "Especially no' after ye and yer men nearly killed one of my best warriors two days past."

Caroline could feel Callum tense behind her. "Mayhap ye'll want to stop stealing sheep and cattle from MacMoran land if ye dinnae like being brought to task for it, then."

The air suddenly grew thick with aggression. Several of MacBean's men shifted in their saddles and brought their hands to their sword hilts. In response, the MacMoran warriors around her did the same, muttering about bastard MacBeans.

Oh shit. Caroline was about to be in the middle of

another battle—one that had nothing to do with her and her mission to get back to her own time.

This was all too much. Falling through time. Losing her sisters. Getting kidnapped and held hostage in a medieval castle. And now she was probably going to die in some stupid fourteenth-century clan war without ever finding Hannah and Allie again.

No. This was not how things would end. To hell with Callum. To hell with 1394. To hell with it all. Caroline was going back to her own time, and back to her sisters, damn it.

As the tension around her continued to mount, her gaze shot to the loch. Maybe it was some sort of portal to Leannan Falls, or to the present day. There was only one way to find out.

Just as Callum opened his mouth to speak, Caroline drove her elbow straight into his ribs. Whatever he'd been about to say turned into a grunt and he started to fold over her. She only had a heartbeat of opportunity. She used it to slip from the horse's back.

She bolted straight for the loch, Callum's plaid falling away from her shoulders as she ran. She heard a commotion behind her, but she didn't bother looking back. Callum and the others would probably catch her in another twenty feet, but that didn't matter because the loch was only ten feet away.

Caroline plunged into the shallows, paying no heed to the rocks biting into her slippered feet below the surface. She plowed deeper, her wool skirts dragging heavily as they became waterlogged.

When the water reached her chest, she dragged in a deep breath, said a prayer to whatever god or demon or spirit had sent her here, and dove under.

Chapter Six

"What the bloody hell is going on?" Laird MacBean murmured in Gaelic under his breath.

Callum wouldn't mind knowing the answer to that, either. He sucked in a lungful of air against his aching ribs and swung down from his saddle.

"Laird, do ye want us to—"

Callum held up a hand to cut Bron off. "Nay. I'll fetch her." *Again.*

As he began to tromp toward the loch, Laird MacBean called, "Is that dunderheaded lass a MacMoran, Laird?"

"I thought she was a MacBean," Callum muttered through clenched teeth.

MacBean's gaze fixed on Caroline and he lifted an eyebrow as she began splashing into the water. "Never laid eyes on the likes of her before."

With a curse, Callum picked up his pace. *Damn it all.*

47

Not only had his plan to trade the lass to MacBean in exchange for a temporary truce just fallen apart, now he was stuck with the addle-brained woman.

The addle-brained woman who had just dived completely underwater.

Cursing again, Callum tossed aside the plaid on his shoulder and strode into the loch. He didn't bother removing his boots or trews, for if the lass had a death wish, the cold waters could claim her before he'd finished.

He waded to where she'd ducked under and began fishing with his hands for her. In only a few moments, he bumped into her arm. He clamped his fingers around her and dragged her up. She broke the surface, sputtering and sucking in breath.

Shoving the wet veil of dark hair from her face, she blinked. Her eyes focused on him, then shifted to the waiting group of MacMorans and MacBeans.

Despair swept over her delicate features like a storm cloud.

"Nothing happened. It didn't work."

"Aye, of course no', ye daft woman," Callum snapped. "This is just a loch, no' some magical gateway to a waterfall near Edinburgh or the future or wherever the hell ye think ye're going."

He scooped her up, and though she was slight, the weight of her waterlogged wool gown made his progress back to the shoreline slow. As he stomped toward his horse, he bent and scooped up first his discarded plaid and then hers, muttering all the way about water in his boots and wet trews that were bound to chafe on the ride back to Kinmuir.

By the time he reached the others, her teeth had begun to chatter, though he wasn't sure if it was from the cold loch waters or shock that her attempted escape had failed.

He set her on her feet beside his horse and grudgingly wrapped both plaids around her. At least she stood docilely rooted in place as he remounted and pulled her up across his lap. Mayhap her impromptu dunk in the loch had taken some of the fight out of her.

When he was settled once more, he found Laird MacBean watching him with those too-keen eyes.

"Ye said ye thought the lass was a MacBean," the Laird said, his voice overly calm. "Let me guess—*she* is the matter ye wished to discuss with me. Ye thought to trade her back to me in exchange for—what? Coin? Grain?"

"Peace," Callum replied through gritted teeth. "A promise from ye to leave my lands and people alone."

Laird MacBean stiffened, his eyes narrowing. "What ye now call *yer* land belonged to the MacBeans for generations."

"That doesnae give ye the right to raid and terrorize the MacMorans who peacefully live here now," Callum shot back. He drew in a breath to calm his rising anger. "My father and yers redrew the border decades ago. Both clans agreed to it. Ye have no grounds to go back on that agreement now."

"My people have every right to feed themselves," MacBean bellowed in return.

Just when it seemed that a clashing of swords was inevitable, Terek MacBean placed a hand on the Laird's arm. "Father," the young man murmured.

The simple word brought MacBean back to himself. He huffed a breath, the angry color that had risen to his face abating slightly.

"Yer wee scheme has failed, MacMoran," he said, his temper turning back to shrewd restraint. "The lass is naught to me, so ye have naught to bargain with."

The Laird leaned forward in his saddle then, fixing Callum with a cold stare. "Worse," he went on, "instead of exploiting my weakness, ye've revealed yer own. Yer plan can be used against ye now."

"What is that supposed to mean?" Callum demanded, unease coiling in his gut at the gleam in MacBean's dark eyes.

MacBean lifted his thick shoulders, a coy smile playing around his mouth. "Ye meant to hold something of value against me, but mayhap ye ought to worry that someone might do the same to ye. Take the lass, for example. Ye seem fond of her—fond enough to fetch her from the loch, to wrap her in yer plaid, to hold her close so that she cannae escape again."

Callum realized he was clenching his hands so tight that his knuckles ached. "Is that a threat?" he asked quietly, staring MacBean down.

"Just an observation," MacBean replied casually. "And a warning. I'd be careful if I were ye, Laird. I wouldnae let such a bonny wee thing out of my sight—else someone might find her and do to ye what ye aimed to do to me."

MacBean's eyes slid to Caroline, and Callum fought the urge to draw his sword and run the man through for threatening her. Nay, he had to keep his wits about him. The last thing his clan needed was for him to plunge them into an all-out war with the MacBeans over a lass he hadn't even known two days past.

Still, MacBean's posturing couldn't go ignored. Callum would have to put extra men along their border —men needed for the harvest season, not warfare. Bloody hell, what a mess he was in.

"Is she English, then?" MacBean asked, still eyeing Caroline.

"She *speaks* English," Callum muttered, suddenly feeling weary. "I dinnae ken *what* she is."

MacBean snorted. "Besides daft, ye mean?"

At that, Caroline stiffened in his lap. "I'm not—"

"Hold yer wheesht, woman," MacBean snapped.

The last of Callum's patience evaporated. "I thought ye said ye had no claim to her, MacBean," he growled. "The lass is my responsibility now—which means ye have no place admonishing her. She is under my protection. Threaten her again and find out just what it means to challenge the honor of a MacMoran."

Not waiting for MacBean's reply, Callum dug his heels into his horse's flanks and jerked on the reins, sending the animal careening back toward Kinmuir. His men instantly fell in around him, and they rode hard for home.

Callum nearly lost himself in the rhythm of his horse's long, pounding strides, but he couldn't quite flee a niggling voice in the back of his head.

Aye, Caroline was his responsibility—and he would damn well ensure her safety now that MacBean saw her as a way to strike at him.

But what the hell was he to do with the English-speaking, nonsense-talking, dangerously bonny lass?

Chapter Seven

Once they'd crossed through the castle gates, Callum set Caroline on her feet and dismounted without a word. From the hard set of his jaw and the tightness around his honey-colored eyes, he was furious, but he remained silent, merely taking her by the elbow and guiding her back into the tower.

Caroline held her tongue as well, but not out of anger.

She'd failed. It had been a long shot, but some part of her had held out hope that returning to her own time and reuniting with her sisters would be as easy as simply diving back into the loch she'd appeared in two days ago.

Numb disillusionment threatened to swallow her whole, yet she still had one last chance to get back home. Somehow, she had to convince Callum to let her return to Leannan Falls. That was where this nightmare had begun, and maybe it would end there as well.

She let him pull her up the stairs toward her room, but once they were inside with the door firmly shut behind them, she drew in a breath, gathering her wits.

Yet before she could get the words out, he rounded on her.

"What the hell were ye thinking, jumping in the loch like that?"

She blinked. "I told you already. I need to find my sisters and go back to—"

"No' this nonsense again," he muttered through clenched teeth.

That had her bristling. "I didn't make you come after me, you know."

"Should I have let ye drown, then?"

"I know how to swim."

"Verra well, but ye didnae have the sense to try, did ye? Ye simply sank underwater like a stone."

"I was looking for—"

Caroline's rising voice was cut off when Tilly pushed into the room. The woman's hazel eyes widened as she took in first Caroline's and then Callum's dripping, disheveled appearance.

"Tilly, would ye kindly fetch another of Thora's dresses for Caroline?" Callum said in a tight voice. "In fact, bring all my sister's old clothes—Caroline will be staying here indefinitely."

"What?" Caroline snapped.

Tilly hastily bobbed a curtsy and fled, either to do her Laird's bidding or simply to escape the mounting argument, Caroline wasn't sure which.

She turned back to Callum, matching his cross-armed stance. "I can't stay here. I want to go to Leannan Falls. That's the best chance for me to get back to where I belong."

To her surprise, he let a long breath go and dragged a hand through his wet hair. "I cannae allow that."

"Why not?" she demanded. "It's obvious I'm only causing you problems. If you let me go, then you can get back to…whatever it is you were doing before I got here."

"It's no' that easy. I meant what I said about ye being under my protection now. I cannae spare a contingent of men to escort ye—no' when I need every last one of them either watching our borders or bringing in the harvest. And I cannae simply send ye on yer way alone."

"Why? I've done plenty of backcountry hiking and camping. Just give me a horse and some supplies, and I'll be on my way." An image of riding a horse for a week rose in her mind and she frowned. "On second thought, backpacking my way to the falls might be better."

"What is 'backpacking'?" he asked, scowling.

Caroline exhaled. "My point is, you don't have to be responsible for me. I can take care of myself."

Callum shook his head slowly. "MacBean will be looking for ye. If he comes across ye wandering around the Highlands, he'll take ye and try to ransom ye back to me."

"His threat doesn't hold water, though," she countered. "The only reason he thinks he can use me against you is because he believes I mean something to you—but I don't."

She waited for his agreement, or even just a nod of acknowledgement for the point she'd made, but all he did was stand there like a stone statue before her, his gaze cutting through her and his jaw locked stubbornly.

What the hell did his silence mean? He couldn't possibly be implying that...that she wasn't nothing to him, could he?

Tension crackled like electricity around them as the laden silence stretched. At last, he broke their stare, turning to stand over the flickering embers in the brazier.

"I need to think of my clan first," he murmured. "I cannae risk being manipulated by the likes of Laird MacBean. And I cannae have distractions from my duty."

"And *I* need to get back to Leannan Falls. Won't I be more of a distraction under your nose here at the castle than if you just turned me loose?"

"No' if ye might fall into danger," he replied quietly.

This was like arguing with a rock. What else was she supposed to say to make him see reason? Desperation tightened her throat. What if she was stuck here—in Scotland, in the past, in this damn room—for the rest of her life? What if she never found her sisters again?

Her heart contorted at the thought. It had been one year exactly since she and her sisters had lost both their parents in the blink of an eye. Ever since the car crash, the fear of losing Hannah and Allie had lurked like a monster in the back of Caroline's head.

And now that monster had come to life.

Caroline had always been the "free spirit" of the family, the easy-going one, the one who found the fun and adventure in every situation. But behind her laid-back façade, Caroline was still just the baby of the family, both to her parents and her sisters. She'd never been without at least one of them looking out for her.

Until their parents had died, she'd always been confident and relaxed—because she'd always had a safety net under her. When she'd left UMaine without a degree and picked up a job as a barista not far from her parents' house in Mayport Bay, she'd known that if things got really bad, she could work in her parents' flower shop, or even move back in with them.

Allie was always around and up for a late-night cookie baking and gab session. And although Hannah had moved out of state years before, her older sister never failed to come through with life advice for the wayward, anchorless Caroline.

But all that had been stripped away, first by the car crash, and then by that damned waterfall. She was alone. An orphan without her sisters to protect her.

Tears burned her eyes as she stood there, feeling helpless and cold. But she couldn't give up. Not yet. Not when there was still a chance that she could get back to her family through the falls.

Swallowing the lump in her throat, she tried again. "You have a sister, right? Thora?"

Callum turned, eyeing her warily. "Aye."

"I take it she doesn't live here anymore, given the

fact that I'm apparently going to take over her old wardrobe."

"She married the Grant Laird's son four years past. Neil takes good care of her and their wee bairn Jamie," he said, his voice gentling slightly.

"Imagine if she just disappeared one day, and you didn't know if she had been kidnapped or killed or what. Wouldn't you do everything in your power to get her back?"

The softness that had briefly loosened his features a moment before disappeared instantly. "Aye, I would."

"Then you can understand why I need to find my sisters. The best chance of that is if I go back to Leannan Falls."

He gave a terse shake of his head, though she didn't miss the way his eyes flashed with regret. "Ye arenae well in the head, lass," he said quietly. "I cannae in good conscience send ye to the falls. If MacBean doesnae catch ye, some other bastard looking to take advantage of ye will."

She stared at him in disbelief. "So you're going to— what? Keep me locked up in this room for the rest of my life? Make me your prisoner forever?"

Callum muttered a curse, raking his fingers through his damp hair again. "I dinnae ken what to do with ye."

Caroline latched onto the single thread of uncertainty in his voice as if it were a lifeline. She racked her brain for something, *anything*, she could say to persuade him that she wasn't crazy, and that he should let her return to the falls.

"What if…" she began, not knowing where she was

headed. "What if I could somehow prove to you that I really am from the future? That I'm not crazy?"

He lowered his dark brows, but he waited for her to go on.

"If I could convince you, would you let me go?"

Amber eyes shining with skepticism, he considered that for a moment.

"Ye wish to strike a bargain, then?"

"Yes," she hurried on. "If I prove to you that I'm not nuts, you'll give me my freedom."

He cocked his head. "Go on."

Shit. Now that she'd finally stumbled upon a way to escape her confinement, she actually had to come up with proof that she'd time-traveled here from the future.

If only her smartphone had traveled back with her. That would convince him quickly enough that she wasn't from this time. But of course she'd left it at the top of the falls with her purse when they'd jumped. There were a million things she could tell him about the future, but he probably wouldn't believe most of it, and she'd come off as even crazier.

Maybe she could tell him something about his own time, but something that could only be known after the fact.

She frantically scanned her brain for all the tidbits of history and trivia she'd learned about Scotland in the last two weeks. A highlight reel of all of Scotland's biggest historical moments flickered through her mind. William Wallace. Robert the Bruce. No, both of those heroes were long gone. The Battle of Culloden hadn't happened yet—and wouldn't for just about three hundred and fifty years. Her bones would be dust long before then.

She needed something closer to 1394. *1394.* Something about the year tickled the back of her brain. Damn it, she should have been paying more attention to all the plaques and markers explaining the history of the places she and her sisters had visited in the last two weeks rather than taking pictures of plants and lochs and the occasional crumbling castle or abbey.

Abbey. Like a piece in a jigsaw puzzle, something snapped into place in Caroline's mind. Dunfermline Abbey. 1394.

"King James I!" She blurted.

"What?"

Caroline drew in a deep breath and closed her eyes, trying to remember every detail about what she'd learned when she and Hannah and Allie had visited Dunfermline Abbey. If she'd known then that her entire life might hang on this one historical footnote, she might not have spent so much time scrolling around on her phone inside the abbey.

"King James I of Scotland is going to be born at Dunfermline Abbey in late July of this year," she said. Her eyes popped open. "Possibly on the twenty-fifth of July."

She looked up to find Callum's wolf eyes narrowed. "I have heard that the Queen Consort carries another of King Robert's bairns."

Caroline snapped her fingers. "Anabella Drummond and Robert III, right?" At Callum's cautious nod, she went on. "Well, she's going to have a boy, and his name will be James."

"But ye called him *King* James," Callum prodded. "Queen Anabella has already borne two male bairns in line for the crown—an heir and a spare."

Caroline hesitated. The reason King James's birth had lingered in her memory was because by the time he was twelve, both his parents and his two older brothers had died. The third son abruptly became the rightful King of Scotland. The idea of a boy so young losing his entire family had saddened and moved her.

But how much should she tell Callum? What were the ethical implications of revealing the future to someone who would live through those events? Did she risk changing the timeline—and therefore the course of history?

Callum was waiting on her answer, his arms crossed over his broad chest.

"He will eventually become King James I," she hedged. "The important part is that Queen Anabella will birth a son, whom she'll name James, on July twenty-fifth."

"That is less than a fortnight from now."

"Yes."

Caroline held her breath as Callum stood considering. At last, he spoke again.

"Verra well. I'll send a missive to Dunfermline to request express notification of the birth of the King and Queen's bairn. Word of the birth of another heir will likely spread quickly, even here in the Highlands, but I dinnae want any of the details lost in transit."

"Thank you," she breathed, her heart rising to her throat. "And when you get confirmation that what I say is true, you'll let me go?"

He rubbed a hand over the bristle on his jawline for a moment. "I'll do ye one better. Ye wish to go to the falls outside of Edinburgh, aye? I'll take ye there myself to ensure yer safe passage."

"Really?" Caroline blurted. "Why?"

"A lass like ye…" Callum's eyes glowed with some unreadable intensity. "Ye shouldnae make such a journey alone—no' with MacBean and all manner of ruffians out there. I willnae allow harm to befall ye." He cleared his throat. "In exchange, however, I'd ask two things of ye."

"What?"

"First, ye'll be permitted free rein of the castle—but ye must agree to stay within the walls at all times. I cannae have ye roaming the Highlands freely with MacBean so keen to take ye for his own aims."

Caroline swallowed. She didn't like the idea of remaining stuck in the castle, but it was better than being locked in this dim, lonely chamber for another two weeks. "Agreed. And your second condition?"

"No more mad attempts at escape." He glared down at his still-wet boots. "Into lochs or otherwise."

To her surprise, Caroline had to repress a grin. "I can agree to that, too—I'll stay within the castle walls and won't try to escape until you get word that James has been born."

"*If*," he said evenly. "No' until—*if* I learn that what ye've said is true."

"You don't believe it's possible, do you?"

He lifted a dark eyebrow. "Nay, I dinnae, but if agreeing to take ye to Leannan Falls when I see pigs fly will buy me a fortnight of peace around the castle, I'd make that promise, too."

She should have been indignant that he'd basically admitted to making a deal he never planned to have to uphold, but hope filled her to brimming, leaving room for nothing else. Two weeks was a long time to be stuck here in medieval Scotland—and a long time to be apart from her sisters without being able to alert them of her safety—but at least now she had a plan.

"I didn't think it was possible, either," she murmured, wrapping her arms around her damp dress. "But then it happened."

"A word of warning, lass."

At Callum's serious tone, she stiffened. "Yes?"

"Dinnae speak as freely with others as ye have with me. I believe ye arenae right in the head—forgive me," he added quickly before going on. "But others...ye speak of moving through time and gateways and predicting births and deaths. Some might call that black magic."

A chill that had nothing to do with her wet clothes raced up Caroline's spine. She didn't have to be a scholar to know what had happened throughout history to women who'd been accused of witchcraft. Sure, the fervor for burning witches wouldn't start for another hundred years or so, but Caroline wouldn't take any chances.

All the more reason she needed to get back to her own time.

Caroline nodded, her throat suddenly too tight to speak.

Callum strode out the door, leaving her alone with a whole new set of fears to consider.

How the hell was she going to survive another two weeks here?

Chapter Eight

Despite the fact that her chamber door hadn't been locked yesterday, Caroline had found herself loath to venture down the stairs. Tilly had kindly brought her a whole trunk of garments, including linen chemises, stockings, indoor slippers, more practical leather half-boots, and several wool gowns dyed in an assortment of colors. Plus, the cook had indulged Caroline's sudden hesitancy and brought food to her room.

But now that she'd gotten a good night of sleep and morning sun streamed in through the open window, Caroline knew she'd done enough wallowing. She had roughly two weeks until Callum would receive confirmation of King James's birth. She didn't plan on spending that entire time hiding in her room like a coward.

She had no idea just how she'd pass the time inside the castle's walls, but there was only one way to find out. Shoving aside her lingering uncertainty, she lifted the skirts of her forest-green gown and marched downstairs.

When she reached the enormous room at the bottom, though, she almost turned tail and fled.

The space bustled with activity. Servers carried trays of steaming porridge, pots of honey, pitchers of milk, and loaves of fresh bread among the overcrowded tables and benches, which had been pulled from the walls into the center of the room. Roughly three dozen men and women ate and talked noisily, oblivious to Caroline.

Until suddenly they all seemed to notice her at once. Heads turned, mouths froze, and eyes swept her curiously. They'd probably all heard about her by now—word of an outsider would spread like wildfire, if medieval castle life was anything like life in small-town coastal Maine.

Caroline scanned the faces of those gathered for the morning meal, but she didn't recognize anyone until her gaze landed on Eagan. She hadn't seen the small-framed, sharp-eyed man since that first day, but with no other familiar faces, she tentatively approached him.

"Eagan, right? I'm Caroline."

The man's mouth turned down behind his neatly trimmed gray and brown beard. He muttered something in Gaelic before grudgingly rising from his bench.

"What do you want, Mistress Caroline?"

"I…um…" Where to start? She wouldn't mind eating, but she would rather get her bearings first. And it would make life easier—even for just the next two weeks —if she knew more than just Tilly, Eagan, and Callum.

"Maybe a tour?" she said, feeling unaccountably nervous under the man's cool blue-gray stare.

"Tilly can look after ye," he said, sounding slightly annoyed. "Come."

Without waiting, he set off at a brisk pace toward the back of the room where the serving girls were going in and out of a swinging door. He pushed through, Caroline hurrying to keep up.

She stepped into a chaos of steaming pots, blazing fires, and a crush of servers and kitchen workers hustling about their tasks. In the center of it all was Tilly, a wooden spoon in each hand and her frizzy red hair billowing wildly around her head.

Tilly was shouting orders to one of the women stirring porridge over the fire, but she cut off her command when her gaze landed on Eagan and Caroline.

"Unless the castle is aflame, I'm busy," she said even before Eagan spoke.

"The lass wants a tour," Eagan said sourly.

"Ye are the seneschal," Tilly replied, dipping one of her spoons into a porridge pot. "It seems to me ye ought to show Mistress Caroline about."

"More important matters fill my time."

Tilly shot him an *oh really* look under lowered eyebrows, but then she sighed. "Margaret, keep an eye on things, dearie. Mind that bread, too. Daughter or nay, I willnae abide burned bread."

Margaret, a woman who appeared to be a younger version of Tilly, bobbed a curtsy and took over the wielding of Tilly's wooden spoons.

Eagan murmured something in Gaelic once again before vanishing through the swinging door.

"What did he say?" Caroline asked.

Tilly wiped her hands on her apron and snorted. "Naught ye need to hear. Suffice it to say that Eagan is verra self-important—so much so that he apparently doesnae feel he needs to abide by the Laird's order to speak English in yer presence."

"But he *can* speak English, obviously," Caroline said, dodging out of the way of a young woman carrying two trays laden with food out of the kitchen.

"Och, aye, we all do." Tilly shot her a wry smile. "The English have given us Scots enough hell over the generations that I suppose we all learned their tongue along the way. Eagan just has a stick up his arse—beg pardon, Mistress."

Tilly pushed her way through the hubbub toward the swinging door, waving for Caroline to follow her. "The rest of the clan will obey the Laird's directive to speak English near ye so that ye arenae left in the dark. But if a certain grumpy seneschal mutters a word in Gaelic now and then, rest assured ye arenae missing much. He just thinks that because he was running this castle for the previous Laird even before our Callum was born, he kens best in all things."

Tilly came to a halt in the big room bustling with the morning meal. "Well now," she said, patting down her hair. "Ye've seen the kitchens and the great hall, so that part of the tour is done."

Great hall. Caroline filed away the word for the massive room they stood in. It sounded vaguely familiar from the various castle tours she and her sisters had gone on, but only now that she had to *live* in a castle for two weeks did she pay attention to the terms.

Tilly guided her up the stairs on the west side of the great hall, pointing out various chambers and storage rooms as she went. She showed Caroline Callum's solar, which was simple and tidily appointed. A wooden desk and matching chair took up much of the space, along with a cabinet for ledgers and writing supplies. The hearth was empty and cold—Callum must not have been in here this morning.

As Tilly took her back through the great hall and to the east tower, curiosity at Callum's whereabouts continued to tug at her. When Tilly halted in front of the landing one floor below Caroline's room and announced, "The Laird's bedchamber," Caroline's stomach did a strange little flip.

He'd been sleeping right below her this whole time? Caroline gave herself a little shake. Why did that matter to her?

Tilly pushed open the door, and to Caroline's horror, she instantly pictured catching Callum in his bed. Maybe he'd be shirtless, the bedding bunched around his lean hips. Maybe he'd pin her with one of those melted-honey stares to see her standing in his bedroom door.

But of course when the door swung open, the chamber was empty and silent. Caroline felt a blush at her ridiculous thoughts rise to her face.

She glanced quickly around the room, noticing the intricate tapestry on one wall, the enormous four-poster bed taking up another, and a large wooden armoire, table, and chair on the third. His chamber had a brazier in one corner, as hers did, but unlike in the solar, embers glowed in the metal grate, a reminder that he'd slept here.

What was more, a faint trace of his scent—soap and smoke and clean male skin—lingered in the chamber. It instantly reminded her of his nearness, of sitting atop a horse in his lap, being wrapped in his plaid.

Belatedly, she realized that Tilly was already bustling back down the spiral stairs. Caroline hastily closed Callum's chamber door and followed the cook, her skin tingling and her cheeks warm with embarrassment over how silly she was being. But when they reached the great hall once more, curiosity got the better of her.

"Where is Callum?" she asked, scanning the hall once more. The meal was already being cleared and those who'd been eating had begun filtering away toward their tasks for the day.

"The Laird is in the yard training with some of the men," Tilly replied. "Come. I'll show ye what's outside the keep."

Caroline followed Tilly out the double doors and nodded along as she was shown the castle's well, the stables, a weapons shed for the castle guards, and a small attached smithy for repairs. But when they stepped around the backside of the keep, her thoughts and attention scattered.

Morning sun glinted off Callum's sweat-sheened bare chest. He stood before a group of a dozen men, some of whom had discarded their tunics as well, yet Caroline couldn't seem to rip her eyes away from Callum. Both of his big hands were closed around a sword. He was walking through a sequence of slow-motion maneuvers which ended in a firm thrust of the blade.

"Again," he said to his men, and they instantly shifted into formation, raising their own swords and moving through the same series of blocks and strikes.

Just then, he turned and his gaze locked on her. In the sunlight, his hair was the rich, dark color of coffee and his eyes sparked like gold. He strode toward her, his sword casually swinging in one hand by his side.

Caroline couldn't help it. She stared.

She'd never seen anyone so good looking in person before—only in movies and on television. Every stacked, sweat-slicked muscle on his torso looked like it had been carved from stone. His broad, corded shoulders and chest tapered to a lean, chiseled waist. His tight-fitted pants—trews, she thought they were called—clung and outlined his powerful legs.

She'd felt his strength when she'd ridden in front of him, her shoulder brushing into the hard wall of his torso, but she hadn't realized just how...*perfect* he was.

When he halted before her, she knew from the masculine grin tugging at his lips that he'd noticed her ogling him. Another unwanted blush rose to her face.

"Are ye getting a tour of Kinmuir, then?"

"Yes," she croaked, then cleared her throat. "Tilly has been kind enough to take time away from her work to show me around."

Callum's brows lowered and he shifted his amber gaze to Tilly. "Eagan ought to have done that."

"Aye, well," Tilly said with a frown and a wave of her hand. "It seemed the seneschal couldnae be bothered this morn. It is no trouble, though, Laird. All that remains for Mistress Caroline to see are the gardens."

Caroline finally managed to tear her eyes from Callum. "Gardens?"

She felt his perceptive gaze on her and got the sense that her sudden interest hadn't gone unnoticed.

"I willnae keep ye, then," he said, turning back to his men. "And remember, Caroline, ye promised to stay inside the castle walls, but ye have free rein within them."

Willing herself not to gawk at Callum's retreating back, Caroline followed Tilly away from the training men.

The two-towered keep sat against the enclosing stone wall on its back side, so there was no way to make a complete circle behind it. Instead they walked in an arc around it, past the doors to the great hall and the closed castle gates in the outer wall opposite the keep.

They came upon a lower stone wall that stood just below head-height for Caroline. It closed off a portion of the space between the keep and the outer wall. Tilly swung open a wooden gate set into the stones and motioned her in.

Caroline blinked at the wild, overgrown garden inside. She would never have guessed that behind all that cold gray stone sat a verdant patch of chaos. Besides one tidy raised bed just inside the wooden gate, the rest looked to have been abandoned.

Fruit trees lined the back of the space, brushing the outer wall and the corner of the keep. Several more raised beds spread out along the ground, all untended and weed-choked. And a wild-looking climbing rose bush had nearly consumed a few trellises propped up against the side of the keep.

Despite the chaotic riot of growth, Caroline was instantly struck by the peacefulness of the place.

"It isnae much at the moment, but I make do," Tilly commented, drawing Caroline out of her silent wonderment.

"What do you mean?"

Tilly huffed a frustrated breath, planting her hands on her hips and eyeing the garden as if it were her foe.

"I ought to have cleared it this spring, but my knees dinnae like bending so much anymore, ye ken. I can keep up this one bed for the kitchen's use, but the rest got away from me."

Caroline nodded thoughtfully. "Would you mind if I helped you get things tidied up in here?"

"*Mind?*" Tilly squawked. "Gracious, nay, mistress, I'd be most grateful!" Tilly beamed, but then her smile faltered ever so slightly. "Ye ken about plants and such?"

Caroline grinned. Finally she'd found something that made sense to her in both the twenty-first and four-teenth centuries. "Yes, I know a bit about plants, and I would love to have something to do around here until—"

Callum's warning against speaking about how she'd fallen through time and was trying to go back flickered across her mind. Yes, it was wise not to go blabbing about time-travel to people who burned witches, but Tilly seemed like the most knowledgeable person in the castle aside from Callum. If there was anyone who could tell her anything else about Leannan Falls or what might have happened to her, it was Tilly.

The cook was waiting expectantly for Caroline to finish her thought.

"…Until I return to my own land," she said. "I'm sure you've noticed that I'm not from Scotland—or England, for that matter."

"I suppose that's none of my business," Tilly replied matter-of-factly. "The way I see it, ye are a guest of my Laird, and that's all I need ken."

"Yes, well," Caroline continued, awkwardly searching for the right words. "When I was…on my way to the Highlands, I passed a place called Leannan Falls. Have you heard of it?"

Tilly's red brows rose slightly. "Och, mayhap, that does sound a wee bit familiar."

"It seemed a very…strange place to me," Caroline plowed on. "Someone nearby told me that the waters were purported to have healing abilities."

"Hmm." Tilly pursed her lips. "I cannae say that I've heard aught about healing waters, but I do remember a legend about that waterfall. Something about a doomed love between a faerie and a man— Leannan means sweetheart, ye ken."

With a wave of her hand, Tilly seemed to brush away her words. "Then again, nigh every falls or mountain or stream in Scotland has a tale to go along with it. Ye ken how the biddies can be with their stories of curses and spells and the like." She paused, fixing Caroline with curious hazel eyes. "Would ye like me to ask the old wives in the village about the falls, mistress?"

Caroline swallowed hard against the pounding of her heart in her throat. Learning more about Leannan Falls might give her some clues about what had happened—or how to get back. But the last thing she needed was an entire village gossiping about the English-speaking loon who might be connected with black magic.

"No," she said reluctantly at last. "That won't be necessary."

Tilly bobbed her head in approval. "That is probably for the best, mistress. Most of those wee battle-axes havenae ever left MacMoran land, so aught they ken will likely just be a mix of rumor and fancy. Besides, we may be isolated and a wee bit superstitious here in the Highlands, but we are still God-fearing folk. It wouldnae be proper to give such tales undue credence."

Caroline could only manage a weak nod. No matter what the villagers around here believed, whatever had happened to her lay beyond comprehension. Maybe some part of Scottish lore was true after all.

Ultimately, it didn't matter one way or the other. All that mattered was that she get back to the falls and find a way home.

Chapter Nine

Callum slipped out the keep's double doors and strode toward the walled garden.

He hadn't seen Caroline yet this morn, but based on the way her eyes had lit up yesterday on her tour of the castle grounds, he had a strong suspicion that he'd find her in the garden.

Tilly had informed him that Caroline had spent much of yesterday gathering tools in preparation for her attack on the overgrown greenery. She'd only come inside for the evening meal, and had been so exhausted that she'd retired immediately to her chamber.

But this morn she was apparently full of energy again, for he'd come down to the great hall to break his fast, only to be told by Eagan that Caroline and Tilly were already outside.

When he reached the stone wall enclosing the garden, he found the wooden gate angled open. Tilly's matter-of-fact voice drifted through it.

"…Fennel over there, and cabbages and carrots next to the lettuces," Tilly was saying.

Callum sauntered through the gate to find the two women's backs to him. Tilly had a wooden spoon in her hand, as she often did, and was pointing at the raised bed at their feet.

"On that end are the peas, beans, and a few radishes and parsnips, though they've gotten a wee bit mixed up in the middle." She shifted her spoon to point at the next bed over. "And somewhere under all these blasted weeds are the turnips, onions, garlic, and leeks."

"I can clear those easily enough," Caroline replied, planting her hands on her slim waist. She wore a simple brown gown and had plaited her hair so that it hung in a dark, glossy rope down her back.

When she'd come upon him training with his men yesterday, his blood had surged hotter than if he'd been in the midst of battle at the look of surprise followed by hunger in her pale eyes. Though he longed to feel the heat of her gaze upon him once more, he was content to observe silently for the time being.

"Aye, I'd be most grateful," Tilly said. "As will all those who eat my cooking—I fear it has become a wee bit bland of late."

"What's in those beds over there?"

Caroline and Tilly ambled farther into the garden, and Callum took the opportunity to lean back against the inside of the stone wall, letting the sun warm his face. He crossed his arms over his chest, his gaze lingering on the delicate sway of Caroline's hips.

She was all gentle curves and coltish energy this

morn. The taut fear she'd exhibited her first few days at Kinmuir had been replaced with an air of relaxed confidence, a comfort in her own skin that he found enthralling.

"The village healer uses these from time to time," Tilly said, using her spoon to wave at two overgrown beds. "I would wager she wouldnae mind if ye cleared them out a bit for her, but mind what's a weed and what isnae." The spoon became an extension of her pointer finger once more. "Dinnae disturb the rosemary, chamomile, St. John's wort, mint, lavender, and the yarrow, else she'll give ye an earful."

"Isn't that foxglove?" Caroline nodded toward a clump of tall stalks with downward tipping pink bell-shaped flowers.

"Och, aye, I forgot. Dinnae clear those either."

"But those are poisonous," Caroline said sharply.

Tilly bobbed her head. "Aye, indeed—in large quantities. But with the right dose, it can calm an erratic pulse and slow a racing heart."

"Medicine or poison, depending on the application," Caroline murmured. "Like just about everything. What about those fruit trees back there?" She lifted her chin toward the back of the gardens, which were cast in deeper shade thanks to the outer wall and the intertwining tree branches.

"Och, ye neednae bother with those, unless ye wish to clean up some of the overgrowth beneath them. Margaret or one of the other lasses from the kitchen see to picking the fruit—apples, pears, and plums." Tilly pointed to each type of tree in the orchard in turn with her spoon.

Caroline strolled down one of the packed-dirt paths between the raised beds and stepped into the dappled shade beneath the trees. "Lovely," she murmured, reaching for a golden speckled pear and brushing it with her fingers.

Callum watched her so intently that Tilly and the rest of the garden seemed to fall away. Mottled sunlight played across her chestnut hair and creamy skin. A faint, happy smile touched her lips as she swept her gaze over the other fruit trees.

What a puzzle she was. When she spoke of falling through time, of appearing out of nowhere at Loch Darraig, of being from the future, Callum was sure she couldn't be in her right mind. But the rest of the time, she seemed perfectly sane.

Perfect.

He silently chastised himself for the foolish word, but as he continued to stare at her, naught else would come to his mind. She was bold and blunt, clever and determined. Yet when she spoke of needing to find her sisters, she revealed a vulnerability that made some deeply male part of him want to protect her from hurt and pain.

And damn it all if her beauty wasn't making him daft. Never before had he beheld such striking features as hers. Those piercing blue eyes could cut through stone, yet the soft curve of her lips were made for kissing.

Bloody hell. Callum gave himself an internal shake. What the hell was getting into him?

Caroline Sutton, it seemed.

Even with all her strangeness, she had a way of wheedling into his thoughts at all hours, heating his blood and making a muddle of right and wrong, real and false.

"Ah, Laird! What are ye doing here?" At Tilly's exclamation, the spell that had closed in around Callum shattered.

Caroline turned, her eyes locking on him, and his stomach did an odd flip. To cover his sudden discomfiture at being caught staring, he pushed off the wall and uncrossed his arms, casually sauntering around the raised beds.

"I thought I'd have a peek at what could keep ye from the kitchens for so long, Tilly."

"Och, I've left far too much to Margaret," Tilly huffed, hurrying past him.

"Nay, yer daughter has things under control," he replied, hoping he hadn't insulted the cook. "Ye've trained her well."

"All the same, I'd best get back. Ye can manage out here for the time being, mistress?"

"Yes, of course," Caroline said with a shy smile. "I'm glad to help."

Tilly hustled through the garden gate and to the small side door leading to the back of the kitchens, which gave the cook easy access to her ingredients.

When the door closed behind her, Callum's guts did another wee dance. Once again, he was alone with

Caroline.

He cleared his throat. "I'm glad ye've found something to occupy yer time here."

She ducked her head and shrugged. Moving to one of the most unruly beds, she sank down onto her haunches and picked up a trowel, setting to work clearing out the weeds.

"I studied this stuff, you know—plants, I mean. But I think I made the mistake of trying to turn something I love into my job."

Callum frowned. Several portions of what she'd just said didn't make sense to him. She dipped in and out of that sort of perplexing talk with such ease that it almost seemed normal.

For a fleeting moment, he considered the possibility that she truly *had* come from the future. Plenty of people still believed in the old magic. Was it so far-fetched to imagine that some spell or curse had brought her here?

It was a strange thought for a man who valued logic and level-headedness, who put far less credence in words and ideas than he did in actions. A man was only as good as his deeds, after all.

Once again, Caroline was making a muddle of his normally orderly thoughts. Still, no matter how much he challenged the lass, she maintained her insistence that this tale about falling through time was true. Mayhap instead of fighting her, he ought to listen to her more to see if he could make sense of what she meant.

He moved to her side and lowered himself into a crouch, eyeing the assorted spades, rakes, and hoes lying on the ground. When he selected a trowel like hers and began digging out the weeds as she was, he felt her cast him a curious, sidelong glance.

"First of all, what do ye mean, ye studied plants?"

Now he was gifted with her full, piercing stare. She hesitated for a moment, but then with a faint smile, she resumed her work on the bed.

"In my time, women can go to universities just like men. I studied botany for a little while, but it was…let's just say I didn't like all the math and chemistry. So I switched to sustainable agriculture—how to grow crops so that the land stays healthy."

He chewed on that for a moment, deciding to accept what she'd said without comment.

"And what do ye mean by turning what ye love into a job?"

Her brows creased as she considered how to answer. "You're the Laird of the MacMorans, which means it's your job to take care of your people—give them protection, help them if they fall on hard times—and in return they work the land and give you part of their harvest, right?

"Aye, close enough."

"Well, in my time, I don't have a Laird, so I have to work to earn money to pay for things like where I live and food and stuff like that. I thought I could do that by studying plants, but doing so ended up taking away the joy I got from it, if that makes sense. I like being outdoors. I like making things grow. And I like getting my hands dirty."

To demonstrate her words, she held up one of her

soil-covered hands and shot him a grin. "But it turns out I don't like doing it for money."

"What *did* ye do to earn money, then?"

"I was a barista."

"What is a…*barista*?" The word felt strange in his mouth.

Her lips curved up again. "It's someone who serves drinks."

He frowned. "Like a serving wench in an alehouse?" For some reason he didn't like the image that rose to his mind of her pouring ale in a dank, smoky tavern surrounded by men with roaming hands.

"Not exactly," she replied. "The drinks are made out of a kind of bean."

"Drinks made of *beans*?"

At his disbelieving tone, she laughed. The sound, sudden and sweet, made his ribs compress against his lungs.

"Suffice it to say, I wasn't an ale wench, but it wasn't the best of jobs, either. It paid the bills—barely—but I never liked it much. I was kind of just…coasting. Not living up to my potential, according to Hannah and Allie."

At the mention of her sisters, Caroline fell into somber silence, which Callum didn't wish to disturb. They continued to work side by side, yet Callum felt acutely aware of Caroline's every motion, every shift and breath.

"I can't believe you have this little oasis of crazy chaos in the middle of these stone walls," she said eventually, leaning back on her heels to rest for a moment. "It's so lovely in here."

He lifted an eyebrow at her. "The garden isnae for pleasure, ye ken. It's a defense against sieges."

"What do you mean?"

He used his trowel to motion toward the beds Tilly used for the kitchen. "If an enemy set upon us, they could seal us in, preventing us from getting fresh water or supplies for months—years, even."

Caroline's eyes widened. "*Years?*"

"Aye. They could starve us out, wait until every last one of us was dead before claiming the castle for themselves. That is why we have a well within the castle walls. And this garden protects us from the threat of starvation."

"Has that happened recently? A siege, I mean?"

"No' in my lifetime, thank God," he replied, "but when my father first became Laird, it did."

Her riveted, concerned gaze made him hurry to add, "Luckily, no one starved, in part because the Campbells couldnae continue the siege, but this garden kept the castle's inhabitants well fed for several months."

She glanced admiringly around the garden, but then gave him a sideways look. "Hmm. I'm glad it ended well, but I'm not sure I agree that this garden is purely for defensive purposes." She pointed at the climbing rose that had nigh taken over the keep on this side. "You can't tell me *that* is for protection."

To his surprise, he felt a rueful smile lifting his mouth. "Fair enough. My mother planted it many years past for its beauty alone." Though she had died nearly ten years ago, a dull ache at her loss warred with the warmth in his chest at the fond memory of her.

Caroline must have sensed his mood, for she remained silent for a long moment. "A garden is never only one thing," she murmured.

He considered that as he eyed the climbing rose. He'd always been more like his father, seeing the practical uses of things rather than their aesthetic value. Yet his mother had once delighted in this corner of the castle not for its utilitarian purpose, but for the pleasure it gave.

"I suppose even in a garden designed for sustenance, the nose can also delight in fragrance, and the eye can find pleasing beauty as well," he conceded.

He turned to find her staring at naught, her eyes distant and glazed with tears.

"Beauty for beauty's sake," she said, her voice squeezing with emotion. "My parents always said that."

"Caroline?"

Without thinking, he moved closer, until his spread knees nearly bracketed her. He quickly swiped the dirt from his hands onto his trews, then reached for her face, cupping one cheek in his palm.

He tilted her face so that he could read her eyes. They were pinched with pain and filled with tears. "What's wrong, lass?" he murmured, his brows knitting.

"It's—" She swallowed hard, shaking her head. A single tear slipped down one cheek, and she swiped at it with the back of her hand. But she left a smudge of dirt where she'd touched her skin.

Gently, he raised the edge of the plaid hanging over

his shoulder and brushed it against her cheek. "Whatever it is, tell me so that I may ken what to do to make it right."

A sad smile touched her lips, but she shook her head again. "There is nothing to be done. They're gone."

Another tear trailed down her cheek. He knew what it meant to lose one's parents. Aye, he couldn't take away her pain, but he didn't like to see her cry, either. He used his thumb to wipe away the tear, smoothing it over her velvety skin.

"Come now," he murmured. "Would they want ye salting this perfectly fine soil with yer tears?"

A weak, wobbling laugh rose in her throat, and the sound once again shot straight through his chest like an arrow.

"No," she conceded.

She stilled then, her gaze locking with his. Callum realized he was still touching her. He held her face cupped in one hand, his thumb slowly swishing over her creamy cheekbone.

A slow breath slipped from between her lips as her eyes roamed over his face, settling on his mouth.

His own breath froze in his lungs. *Bloody hell and damnation*. He was about to kiss her. And he couldn't stop himself. Like a moth to flame, he moved closer until he could feel the heat of her mouth only a hair's breadth away.

"Laird!"

At the sound of Eagan's voice in the garden's entryway, Callum jerked back as if he'd been burned.

Caroline exhaled sharply, blinking as if waking from a dream.

Rising abruptly to his feet, Callum spun to find Eagan standing inside the gate. From his pinched mouth and the steady, cool gaze he was giving Callum, Eagan had seen enough to know what had almost just happened.

"Laird, several missives require yer attention," Eagan said stiffly. "And Bron is asking about a change in the guards' rotation on the south wall."

"Aye," he said, dragging a hand over his face. "I'll speak with Bron first, then I'll meet ye in the solar."

He turned back to her and their gazes tangled.

"Forgive me," he murmured.

"There's nothing to forgive."

Though a blush sat on her cheeks and her voice was breathy with surprise, the earnestness in her eyes told him that she meant the words. Still, he felt like a damned arse for almost kissing her and then leaving her so suddenly.

But he couldn't turn his back on his responsibilities. He followed Eagan out of the garden, steeling himself against the mad urge to go back where Caroline sat amongst the weeds and dirt and flowers and claim her lips with his.

Chapter Ten

Caroline wiped the sweat from her brow with one arm. She fleetingly imagined dumping the bucket of cool water she held over her head instead of onto the raised beds before her.

Even though she'd selected a lightweight gown of buttery yellow, the day was warm and sunny, and she'd been hauling water most of the morning. But she didn't mind—the beds she'd so arduously cleared needed the water more than she did.

Amazingly, it hadn't rained for a full week—not since the day Callum had almost kissed her here in the garden. The memory stirred a warmth in the pit of her stomach that had nothing to do with the sun overhead.

Unrest had hounded her this past week. The almost-kiss had left her breathless and wanting—and impatient to find out what his lips would feel like against hers. She hadn't meant to get emotional in front of him, but he'd been surprisingly tender, and then—

And then Eagan had shown up, and Callum couldn't get away fast enough. From the way he'd kept his distance since then, he either felt guilty for nearly kissing her, or he wasn't interested.

But no, she'd seen desire burning in his amber eyes that day. Yet something was keeping him away. He had usually eaten breakfast and gone to either his solar or the yard to train with his men by the time she entered the great hall every morning, and he often quickly ate the evening meal alone on the raised dais before retiring for the night.

She wouldn't have minded if he'd made another move on her. Once word arrived in a little over a week that King James had been born, she'd be headed to Leannan Falls—and hopefully her own time. So what was the harm in making out with a gorgeous Highland Laird while she waited? Yet they'd exchanged nothing but a few words in the last week, none of them about the almost-kiss.

With no other outlet for her restlessness, Caroline had thrown herself into tending the garden. It had taken several days of hard work just to clear the beds, tidy up the orchard, and prune the climbing rose back a bit.

When that was done, she'd feared she would have nothing to do but sit in her chamber thinking about her sisters and Callum and how the hell she'd gotten here, but luckily Tilly had been willing to let Caroline take over the gathering of vegetables, fruits, and herbs for the kitchen.

They'd set up a routine of sorts. Tilly would leave a basket outside the door leading to the back of the kitchen each morning, and Caroline would fill it with everything that was ripe and ready to be picked from the garden.

When Tilly was done overseeing the morning meal, she'd collect the basket and incorporate whatever Caroline had harvested into the rest of the day's food. And Caroline would spend her time watering, plucking the stray weed, or smoothing the pathways between the beds with a rake. Tilly was grateful not to have to bend on achy knees over the garden each day, and Caroline was glad to have something to keep her busy, something that gave her a sense of purpose during her time here.

Truth be told, it had been a while since she'd felt so useful. Sure, people back home liked to have their coffee made just so every morning, and she was a good barista, but this was bigger than that. She was using her love of nature and what she'd learned about plants to grow things and feed people.

And she'd given the residents of Kinmuir Castle their garden back. Margaret and some of the other girls from the kitchens had begun visiting the garden, shyly smelling the climbing roses and gathering petals for sachets and soap.

A boy of perhaps ten who worked in the castle stables had even approached and somberly asked Caroline's permission to pick a few of the wild bluebells and white clover she'd intentionally left in one of the beds. He wished to give them to a lass he fancied. Of course she'd agreed, trying not to grin as he'd hurried away with his little bundle of flowers in search of his sweetheart.

So although she was currently hot and a little sore from all her efforts this past week, it was more than worth it. Now if only she could occupy her mind as well as she'd occupied her body, then she might finally be able to banish Callum and that damn almost-kiss from her thoughts.

She emptied the last of the water onto the tender shoots of parsnip and carrot greens, then headed through the garden gate toward the well on the other side of the yard, the bucket swinging loosely in her hand. But just as she reached the well, a loud groan and squeal of metal had her head snapping up.

The guards on the wall above the castle's entrance were ratcheting up the portcullis and opening the gates. Confused, Caroline glanced around. Her gaze landed on the stables tucked against the wall. The wooden doors were open and a few stable lads were leading saddled horses out into the yard.

Just then, the keep's doors opened as well, and a half-dozen MacMoran men poured out. Followed by Callum.

Caroline froze, her stomach pinching at the sight of him. As usual, he wore fitted trews tucked into tall leather riding boots. But thanks to the warmth of the day, he had on only a loose white linen tunic. The sleeves were rolled back to reveal bronzed forearms corded with muscle and lightly dusted with dark hair.

As he strode toward the stables, his amber eyes locked on her, and her insides did another somersault. He slowed, letting the others stream past her toward the waiting horses.

"Ye could ask one of the lads to help ye carry water, ye ken," he said, frowning at the bucket in her hand.

She couldn't help feeling a little defensive at that. She'd been working hard this past week, and all he had to say was that she could get a stable boy to help her?

"I don't mind," she said coolly, setting the bucket at her feet.

He remained silent for a moment, his gaze traveling over her face. "Ye are on everyone's lips of late."

"What?" she squeaked, completely caught off-guard. Unbidden, her eyes locked on his mouth. Her mind instantly went back to that moment when he'd been close enough to kiss her.

"They cannae stop speaking of what ye've accomplished in the garden," he went on. "Yer hard work has been much praised."

Had he read her mind when she'd bristled a moment before? While she fumbled for words, he added, "I am grateful for all ye've done, but I dinnae like the thought of ye coarsening yer hands or straining yer back carrying water when one of the lads could aid ye."

"Oh. Well. Um, thank you," she managed, feeling a blush surface on her cheeks. Apparently despite his distance over the last week, he'd noticed her efforts and was concerned for her comfort. That sent an unexpected flutter coursing through her.

"Where are you going?" she blurted as he began to turn away. She waved at the open gate and his waiting horse. "Not another skirmish with the MacBeans, I hope."

"Nay," he said, fixing her with eyes that reminded

her of warm honey. "Only to repair a few thatch roofs and check on the eastern border."

"Ah." She gazed past him out the open gates. It had been a joy to be surrounded by plants this past week, yet the sweeping expanse of grassy hills and the darker forests beyond drew her like a magnet. The castle was big, but not big enough for someone who was used to spending every weekend roaming in forests and mountains without roads, telephone poles, or buildings in sight. "That must be…nice."

"Ye arenae thinking of making a break for it, are ye, lass?" His low, teasing voice was close, and she realized with a start he'd drawn nearer as she'd been gazing out the gates. "Because I *will* catch ye."

She huffed a breath that was part-laugh, part-nervous exhalation at the way her skin tingled at his words.

"No," she replied, glancing sideways at him. "I promised I wouldn't try to escape again, and I'm good for my word. I'm just going a bit stir-crazy, that's all."

His brows drew together at her choice of words, but apparently the meaning came across, for he followed her gaze through the gate. He seemed to consider something for a long moment, a frown on his features.

"Ye wouldnae be interested in coming along, would ye?"

"What?"

"Ye've earned my people's respect this past sennight," he replied evenly. "Ye've worked tirelessly for their benefit. Yet it seems ye arenae used to being confined inside stone walls. Would ye like to join us on our ride?"

Caroline felt her eyes widen and her mouth fall open. "Oh, *yes!*"

He fixed her with a stern look. "We arenae going anywhere near Loch Darraig, ye ken, so dinnae start plotting another wee swim. And I willnae give ye yer own horse in case ye get some mad idea about trying to bolt off again."

"Of course," she said quickly. "I don't really know how to ride anyway. But I would love to go with you."

"Just to see a wee bit of the countryside."

"Yes."

"And get some fresh air."

"Exactly."

Apparently satisfied by her answers, his guarded look eased slightly. "Verra well." He turned to his waiting men, who sat atop their horses curiously watching their Laird. "The lass is coming along. She'll ride with me."

Callum ignored the surprised murmurs from the warriors, instead swinging onto his horse's back and extending a hand toward her. He lifted her easily onto the saddle in front of him, settling her across his lap.

As he nudged the horse into motion and they passed through the gates, a surge of excitement rose in her throat and made her breath catch—though how much was from the sprawling wilderness in front of her and how much was from Callum's powerful arms looping around her to hold the reins, she couldn't say.

Chapter Eleven

C allum jumped down the last few rungs of the wooden ladder and landed agilely beside the humble cottage.

Caroline watched from the shade of a copse of trees nearby as he clasped forearms with the elderly man whose roof Callum and the other MacMoran men had just repaired.

That morning, they'd ridden east across lush hills and past sparkling lochs as Caroline clung to Callum, learning the rhythm of the horse's strides in his arms. When they'd reached the base of a ridge of towering, craggy mountains that left Caroline in awe, they'd turned southward to trail along the MacMoran border.

As the mountains tapered back to hills in the southeast corner of Callum's land, they'd turned toward the castle once more, but instead of going directly back, they'd made several stops at remote, humble cottages like the one they were at now.

Most were inhabited by older clanspeople who didn't have children or neighbors to help them, though they'd also stopped at a hut where a young widow and her two small children lived. Bron, in particular, had gone out of his way to help the woman by chopping firewood, hauling water, and shoveling out the stalls in her small stable, all while wearing a blush at the other men's gentle teasing.

Callum had insisted that Caroline needn't help when the men repaired thatch roofs or mucked out stalls, but she'd made each of the widow's two young daughters a garland of wildflowers to wear in their hair as she'd watched the MacMoran men work.

All those they visited seemed genuinely moved and humbled to receive their Laird's attention and help, yet none were stunned at his unexpected arrival. Caroline suspected that was because the MacMorans were used to seeing their Laird roll up his sleeves and work along with everyone else who was able. Warm respect expanded inside her until she felt ready to burst as Callum accepted the old man's thanks and grasped his forearm once again.

As the others remounted and called their farewells to the old man, Callum approached her where she sat in the shade.

"That was our last stop before the castle," he said, extending a hand to help her rise. His palms were warm, his fingers callused and strong around hers. His grip loosened, but he didn't release her hand even once she was standing. "I hope ye've enjoyed the excursion."

"I truly have," she murmured. "This land...and your people..."

She let a breath go, unsure how to put into words all the feelings swirling inside her. Respect. Wonder. *Longing*...

He flashed her a rare, proud smile, then guided her back to his waiting horse. "Ye arenae the first to be left speechless by this place."

Once he'd mounted, he lifted her into his lap. The position was beginning to feel wonderfully familiar.

With a whistle to his men, they set off at a brisk pace, riding into the sloping afternoon sun. Caroline drank in her surroundings as if she'd just walked across a desert. She'd been moved by Scotland's beauty on her trip with her sisters, yet it was not only this place, but this *time* that reverberated like a struck tuning fork within her.

As far as her gaze would reach, Caroline could see no highways, no buildings, no cars—nothing but sprawling green wilderness all around. Birds flitted low over the grassy hillsides, swirling up into the clean, pure air and darting off toward the trees in the distance. The drone of cars and the muted rumble of airplanes were gone. No noise except for the hoof-falls of their horses and the occasional snort or creak of leather filled her ears.

Callum must have noticed her intense interest in everything around them, for he leaned forward and murmured in her ear as they rode.

"Ye see those peaks?" He pointed toward a cluster of three mountains far off to the north.

At her nod, he continued. "It is said that two men from warring clans fought over one woman there. When she couldnae take their squabbling anymore, she turned them both to stone, but she accidentally made herself into a mountain as well, freezing them all together for eternity."

She gazed at the mountains. The one in the middle was smaller than the two flanking it, and if she squinted, she could imagine each of the taller peaks trying to tug the middle peak away.

At her soft chuckle, he shifted his arm to point at a ribbon of water that meandered between the hills to their left. As he spun a tale about mystical horse spirits who were said to guard the river, she leaned back against his chest, letting his deep, rich brogue wash over her.

Something seized in her heart as she listened to Callum and stared in wonder at her surroundings. Her parents had always meant to visit Scotland someday. When someday had never come and the car crash stole them away, Caroline and her sisters had made a pact to come here to experience what their parents never had.

The dull, familiar ache—for her parents, and now for her sisters as well—began beating in her chest like a painful pulse, and her eyes pricked with tears. Though she and Hannah and Allie had sought to absorb all they could on this trip as a way of honoring their parents, it felt wrong to be so taken with this place now, after they'd all been torn apart.

As if she were betraying not only her parents, but also her sisters.

In the deepest corner of her heart, Caroline knew—

some small part of her wanted to stay here. She was falling for this place, this time—this man.

What kind of selfish, awful sister did that make her? For all she knew, Allie and Hannah had surfaced in the pool below Leannan Falls only to discover that she had vanished. Knowing her oldest sister, Hannah would have likely called every authority demanding a full investigation, and Allie would make herself sick with worry and grief.

Now that their parents were gone, they only had each other. And here Caroline was, letting herself be enchanted by the beauty of the Highlands, the unexpected, simple pleasures of this era, and a Highland Laird who was equal parts rugged stone and warm man.

Things were almost too good here. But she couldn't let herself be distracted from her goal—to get back to Leannan Falls, and hopefully the present. Even if some selfish part of her wanted to stay, she couldn't give in to it.

But another creeping fear rose in her mind. What if she could *never* get back? What if her tumble through time had been a one-way trip? Could she ever be happy here, knowing that she'd never see her sisters again?

Her stomach twisted at the thought. But she wasn't sure which terrified her more—never being able to go home again, or how much she found herself wanting to stay.

Belatedly, she realized she'd gone stiff against Callum, her hands balling so tightly in her lap that her knuckles were white.

She glanced up to find him watching her, his amber eyes clouded with concern.

"Where did ye go just now?"

She shook her head, trying to clear the storm of confusing emotions from her mind, but her throat was tight when she spoke. "I don't know. I got lost, I guess."

Callum's gaze softened. "I want to show ye something." He lifted his voice to the others. "I'm taking Caroline to the stones. The rest of ye return to Kinmuir. We'll be back before the evening meal."

The men shot surprised looks at each other. "Are ye sure, Laird?" Bron asked, his brows raised and one side of his mouth beginning to curve up. "Ye already ken the wee lass is a slippery one. If the two of ye are alone, ye might have to hold her close to keep her from escaping again."

Callum pinned him with a withering look. "Shut yer flap unless ye'd like me to shut it for ye, Bron. We will see ye back at the castle."

"Aye, Laird," Bron said deferentially, but a grin still played at the corner of his lips. With a whistle, Bron set the others into a trot, headed toward the castle.

As the rumble of their hooves faded, Callum's thighs stiffened beneath her.

"Hold on, lass," he murmured in her ear.

When she looped her arms around his torso, he dug in his heels, and they took off at a gallop.

Chapter Twelve

Callum should never have taken Caroline out of the castle.

Mayhap he shouldn't have even scooped her up beside Loch Darraig in the first place.

And he sure as hell shouldn't be taking her to the standing stones in the woods south of Kinmuir Castle.

His life would be a hell of a lot simpler if he hadn't done any of those things.

But it was too late.

From the moment he'd first laid eyes on Caroline, Callum had felt an inexplicable pull toward her. Aye, at first he'd only thought to use her to bargain for peace with the MacBeans, but after that had proven a failure, he'd allowed himself to grow curious about her.

He'd let that curiosity bud into something more—interest, followed by respect and protectiveness. *And desire.*

Still, he'd been safe until that morning, when he'd

seen the way her face lit up at the prospect of venturing outside Kinmuir's walls. It had hit him like a blow to realize that he could give her happiness—*wanted* to give her happiness, more than he wanted to abide by his rules and principles.

And now that her thrilled laugh filled his ears, her arms wrapped tight around him as they tore across the open moors, there was no going back. He wanted her.

It was madness to be alone with her now. He'd spent the entire day watching her surreptitiously. And not because she'd given him reason to believe she might attempt to escape—she hadn't. Nay, he simply couldn't stop himself.

As she drank in their surroundings, he felt as though he were seeing the world for the first time through her eyes. Her wonder, her awe, her reverence for this land that had forged him, made his heart swell with pride against his ribs.

But more than that, *she* captivated him. Her enthusiasm was infectious, turning what could have been a grueling day-long chore into a grand adventure. The scent of her, all wildflowers and sun-warmed earth, drifted around him like a delicate embrace as they'd ridden, making his head spin.

And he'd nigh fallen from Auld Rabbie MacMoran's roof at least twice because he couldn't stop stealing glances at her. The sun and wind had touched her cheeks, leaving them rosy. Wild wisps of chestnut hair had flown from her braid to frame her delicate features. Aye, the magnificence of his lands paled in comparison to her intoxicating beauty.

With his blood running hot and his senses over-whelmed by Caroline's nearness, it wasn't wise to take her to the stones. But to hell with wise. Every decision he'd made since becoming Laird had been for the betterment of his people. Just this once, he wanted to be selfish—he wanted *more* of her.

Nay, he wasn't so far gone that he would throw away everything he and his clan had fought for. He couldn't touch her. But at least he could have her to himself for a few blessed moments.

As they rode into the cool, quiet forest, Callum slowed his horse. Caroline lifted her head but didn't loosen her hold around his middle.

"What are these stones you're taking me to?" she asked, her breaths still short from their exhilarating ride.

"Ye'll see." He guided the horse deeper through the trees until they reached a gurgling stream. He followed it south, winding along the forest floor.

When the trees thinned slightly, he knew they were there. Reining the animal to a halt, he swung out of the saddle and lifted Caroline down after him. He let the horse amble to the stream for a drink and took Caroline's hand, pulling her toward the little clearing.

She halted abruptly when they reached the outer ring of stones.

"What...what is this?"

He watched her, trying to imagine what this place must look like through her eyes. The pines and oaks cleared around a circle of upright stones that stood well over Callum's head. Inside the first ring was a second circle of stones, these ones offset and slightly shorter.

A few of the stones listed, and two had even toppled over. Most had cracks and were covered with moss. Callum had studied them closely enough to know that some had the faint traces of etchings and carved markings on them, though the elements had smoothed them to illegibility.

"They are standing stones," he said, stepping closer and running a hand along one of the slabs. "Long before this land was Christian, people followed the old ways."

"My sisters and I saw something like this on our trip," Caroline murmured, staring wide-eyed. "Though six more centuries of wear and tear made them a bit more rubble-like than these ones."

"I like to come here when I need to think." He extended his hand to her. "Come."

"Oh no," she said with a shake of her head. "Leannan Falls was enough for me. The last thing I need is to step into some mystical stone circle and fall even *further* back through time."

Though he still didn't put much faith in the mad notion that what she said about being from the future was true, he couldn't help but chuckle at that. "I've been here dozens of times, and I've never opened any strange portals or traveled to another era."

She eyed his hand warily, but after a long moment, she took it, grudgingly letting him lead her into the center of the ring.

Their fingers intertwining, they stepped into the middle of the stones and stood side by side, motionless. Callum could feel Caroline's heartbeat where her wrist touched his. Of its own accord, his pulse, steady and strong, slowly came to match hers. Their breaths lengthened and deepened in rhythm together.

The noises from the forest—the soft rustle of leaves and pine needles, the occasional chirp of a bird, the bubbling of the stream that ran along one side of the stone circle—seemed to grow distant. It felt as though all that was left of the entire world was the two of them and the stones.

When he glanced at her several minutes later, he found her eyes wide and her lips parted with wonder.

"Ye see? Ye're still in one piece and we havenae fallen through time—at least I dinnae think we have," he said with a teasing grin, breaking the delicate spell hanging around them. He guided her out of the circle and into the shade of the trees where the stream came closest to the stones.

"Have some water if ye like. I'll fetch us something to eat."

Caroline moved to the stream and cupped her hands in the clear water while Callum went to his horse. He dug out a length of plaid from one saddlebag and a canvas-wrapped bundle of food in the other. Giving silent thanks for the fact that Tilly wouldn't let any MacMoran leave the castle without packing at least two days' worth of food along with them, Callum carried the plaid and bundle back toward Caroline.

He arranged the plaid on the forest floor between the stream and the edge of the stones, under the shade of the spreading boughs overhead so that Caroline's delicate skin didn't get any pinker.

When she straightened from the stream, she blinked in surprise at the array of food he'd laid out. Tilly had packed fresh bread, a wedge of white cheese, dried venison, golden pears, and even a wine skin. Callum wondered for a fleeting moment if Tilly had somehow suspected that he might take Caroline away for a private meal, but he set the thought aside as Caroline joined him on the plaid.

As they ate in amiable silence, Caroline's eyes drifted to the stones, her gaze growing distant, as it had just before he'd sent the others back to the castle.

"As I said, I always find that this place helps me think," he commented. "Ye seem to carry a great burden on yer mind. Mayhap speaking of it will help."

She let out a long breath. "I am thinking of my sisters again—and how to get back to my own time."

Callum considered that. He was no healer, so he couldn't be sure if Caroline had suffered a blow to the head or something else entirely, but in the time he'd known her, she'd never once deviated from her story about being from a different time. Nor had her comments about her sisters or her desire to return to Leannan Falls in hopes of finding them ever changed.

Mayhap it wasn't what a healer would recommend, but he decided to go along with what she said without question.

"Ye must love them verra much."

She fixed him with a surprised look. "I do."

"Might it ease yer mind to tell me of them?"

A soft smile came to her lips. "Maybe. I suppose it's worth a try."

She crossed her legs beneath her skirts, her eyes growing warm. "Allison—we call her Allie—is twenty-six. Two years older than me. She's a nurse—a healer, you'd call her. Allie is sweet and kind and loving. Someday she's going to make a great mother, if she could only find the right guy. And Hannah is twenty-eight. She went to a fancy school and became an event planner, a real high-powered CEO-type, which is perfect because she's kind of bossy and overachieving."

Callum let her words pour over him. Though he didn't understand a fair bit of what she was talking about, he could get the thrust of it by watching her eyes and hands, listening to the rise and fall of her voice.

She told tales of squabbles and occasional competition, of fighting over next to naught, only to come to each other's defense when one struggled with a man's betrayal or a setback in their work or studies. Callum listened, smiling to remember all the times he'd tormented his own sister, only to find that now he would kill anyone who thought to harm her.

"…convince our parents to let us get a pet," Caroline went on. "Hannah and I both wanted a cat, but Allie had always wanted a dog. Well, our parents said that until all three of us came to an agreement, there would be no pet."

She shook her head with a grin. "Hannah and I teamed up against Allie, figuring we could bully her into going along with us, given how agreeable she always was. We promised to give her naming rights to any kitten we picked out. And to our surprise, sweet, amenable Allie named the damn cat Kitty just to spite us!"

Callum chuckled. "But yer parents' ploy worked, didnae it? They forced ye to sort it out amongst yerselves."

Caroline's mirth faded and her fingers began fiddling with a few folds of her skirts. "Yes. They were always good about that—keeping us all together, I mean. But like all kids do, we grew up and grew apart somewhat. Allie and I both stayed close to Mayport Bay —our town—but Hannah left for school and never moved back. It took…"

She swallowed hard, but when she continued, her voice was still tight with emotion. "It took our parents' death to really bring us back together. We promised ourselves never to let distance or distractions separate us again. That's what this trip was supposed to be, anyway."

"Yer trip to Scotland, ye mean?" He still didn't know where this land called "America" was, and he'd never heard of Mayport Bay, but Caroline certainly wasn't Scottish.

"Yeah. My parents always talked about traveling here someday. They meant to honeymoon here, or visit on their ten-year wedding anniversary, but it just never seemed to pan out. So after they died, my sisters and I promised to make the trip happen—for them. It's been a year since they passed. Hannah still hasn't moved home, and Allie works a lot—it's better now that she works in a dermatologist's office rather than a hospital, but she's still busy. But we finally stopped putting it off. We wanted to see all the things that Mom and Dad never did, but also spend time together. Make memories. Have adventures."

At that, she gave a rueful snort. "And one hell of an adventure it's turned out to be." She waved vaguely at him, the standing stones, and the horse tethered nearby.

"At least ye'll have a great deal to talk about when ye find them again."

"*If*," she corrected. "*If* I find them again." And just like that, the cloud of sadness and worry that had lifted briefly as she'd talked settled around her once more. "There's no guarantee that I'll be able to go back through the falls. And even if I do, what if Hannah and Allie aren't there when I get back?"

He frowned. What did one say to comfort a woman who believed she'd lost her sisters while journeying through time?

"Family…has a way of finding one another," he offered.

"You don't understand. I've already failed them once. When our parents died, it was so sudden. They were in a car accident." Her troubled gaze flicked to him. "Kind of like a horseback riding accident. We had no warning, no way to prepare. I…I wasn't ready. I didn't step up when I should have. I let them down, and I can't do that again. I can't—"

Her voice broke off on a sob. Without thinking, Callum leaned across the plaid and wrapped his arms around her, pulling her onto his lap.

She buried her face in his tunic, her tears dampening the linen. She felt so small and fragile in his embrace, her shoulders shaking and her breaths coming in stuttering gulps and sobs.

He ran a hand along her spine, murmuring words of comfort and endearment in Gaelic. In all likelihood, she understood him as well as he did when she spoke of car accidents and time travel and making drinks from beans, but he hoped the gist came across.

When she began to quiet, he spoke. "There now, lass. It cannae be as bad as all that."

"You don't know what I did." Her voice was so small that he almost didn't hear her.

His gaze drifted to the stones, which stood silent and accepting before them. No matter what had troubled him, he always felt as though his burden had been lightened after coming to this place. He wanted to give that same relief to Caroline.

"Tell me," he murmured. "And I promise no' to judge whatever ye have to say."

She drew in a deep, shuddering breath. "My parents owned a flower shop. In my time, people pay for cut and arranged flowers to bring to their loved ones."

He nodded, silently encouraging her to go on.

"I used to work summers there when I was in high school. I think everyone in the family assumed that since I already liked plants, I would take over the shop one day. But then 'one day' came too soon, and…and I couldn't do it."

Her hands curled in the front of his tunic and he could hear her swallow, clearly fighting to go on. He only held her, wordlessly willing her to draw strength from him.

"My sisters encouraged me to keep the shop open, in memory of our parents and all they'd built with their little business. They needed me to step up—for the family. To keep the shop alive, and our parents' dreams with it. But I couldn't."

"Why no'?" he prodded gently.

She shook her head against his chest. "That place... I didn't mind it so much before Mom and Dad died, but I've never liked cut flowers. They're beautiful, but they're already dead. I always preferred to plant things, *grow* things. But then after the accident—"

Another sob escaped before she managed to calm herself with a few more deep breaths.

"All I saw in the shop after the accident was *death*. Dead flowers everywhere. Mom and Dad, dead. All their hopes for my sisters and me, for the shop, their dream of visiting Scotland—all gone in the blink of an eye. It was too much. So I bailed. Flaked out. I told Hannah and Allie that I was too busy—being a barista, of all things."

She made a sound that was half snort of disgust, half moan of frustration.

"The truth was, I was terrified," she continued. "Terrified to be an orphan at twenty-three. I couldn't handle it—the responsibility of running the shop, but also the idea of taking over my parents' dreams and goals. I was afraid I'd wither and die in that shop just like all those cut flowers. So we sold the shop. In two weeks, it was no longer ours, and all the flowers inside had died."

"From all ye've told me, yer parents loved ye verra

much," Callum said. "I cannae believe that they would think ye'd failed them in selling the shop."

"Not just my parents. My sisters…they didn't understand. They thought running the shop would be a perfect fit for me, that it would give me structure and purpose. I haven't exactly been the most focused, high-achieving person—not like Hannah and Allie, who both finished school and got real jobs."

She gave a sad chuckle at that before continuing. "But more than that, I think they wanted to keep the shop in the family as a way of remembering Mom and Dad. None of us was ready to lose them. And the shop was a connection to them. It would have eased their grief if I had stepped up and taken over the shop. I let them down."

She lifted her head, fixing him with watery blue eyes. "Which is why I have to get back to them. I didn't do my part to hold our family together once. I can't do that again."

"Ye are a brave one," he murmured, scanning her tear-streaked features. "But ye neednae be so hard on yerself."

She opened her mouth to contradict him, but he went on.

"My mother died ten years past—after a long illness that stole her strength and left her a shadow of her former self. And my father departed this world three years ago with no warning. He had a headache one eve and retired for bed, but he never woke again."

Caroline's eyes widened and her cheeks flushed with embarrassment. "I-I'm sorry for your loss," she murmured, ducking her head against his chest once more. "I didn't mean to blather on about my problems when—"

"Nay, lass," he cut in. "That wasnae a criticism of ye. What I meant was, losing a parent is never easy. Whether it is drawn out or sudden, ye cannae ever be ready for such a thing. But that doesnae make ye a bad person. Mayhap ye didnae react as ye would now, but ye were in the throes of grief then."

He fiddled with a wisp of her dark hair, letting the silky strand slide along his fingers. "I've only kenned ye for a short while," he continued quietly, "but I can say with certainty that ye are a good daughter, and a good sister."

She raised her head again, and this time her gaze was unguarded.

"Have you ever…feared that you've disappointed your family?"

"God, aye," he breathed. "My father left a hell of a mantle to carry. He was a good father and husband, but most of all, he was a good Laird. He always put our people first. When the time came, he wasnae afraid to lift his blade against our enemies, yet more often he fought for peace, for he kenned that a people cannae thrive if they are always at war. I struggle every day to live up to his legacy."

Callum raked a hand through his hair before settling it around Caroline's back once more. *Bloody hell.* He was coming dangerously close to tossing aside prudence and betraying the memory of his father right now.

Some small, sane voice in the back of his mind

screamed that in lingering here alone with Caroline, he was threatening all his father had built, and all he'd continued to work for after becoming Laird. Yet the need roaring through him at Caroline's nearness drowned out the whisper of rationality.

He didn't want to think about duty and responsibility at the moment. He didn't want to think at all. Caroline shifted in his lap, her bottom nestling more fully onto his manhood. Her clear eyes pierced him with a searching look.

The air suddenly felt thick and warm around them. The forest fell away, and he felt as though he was sinking into the pale blue pools of her eyes. She reached up and brushed her fingertips against his lips. He shuddered at the heat that shot through him like lightning—straight to his cock.

"Ever since that day in the garden," she breathed. "I wondered what this would feel like."

The last of his control snapped. He closed the distance between them and claimed her mouth with his.

Chapter Thirteen

A t the first contact of Callum's lips, Caroline melted like ice cream.

It was so much better than she'd even let herself dream in her wildest fantasies. His mouth was soft and gentle at first, the barest brushing of lips. But when she sagged against him, he took control, tilting her back in his arms to deepen the kiss.

She opened to him, and with a feral growl, he found her tongue with his. An answering moan rose in her throat at the velvet heat of his mouth. Their tongues tangled in an erotic rhythm that soon had her breathing fast and hard.

Raw emotion intertwined with the heat lacing her veins. She'd never opened up to anyone about the tangle of guilt and grief left in the wake of her parents' death the way she just had with Callum—not even her sisters. He made her feel safe—safe to be imperfect, to lay her heart bare.

And he made her feel *wanted*.

Beneath her bottom, she could feel the hard length of his cock straining against his trews. He was more than turned on already—and so was she. All the looks and touches they'd exchanged over the course of the day had felt like a long, drawn-out dance that had been leading to this moment.

Yet to her surprise, Callum didn't immediately start ripping her clothes off. Instead, he kissed her, slow and deep, until every inch of her skin burned beneath her gown and she couldn't hold still any longer.

She shifted restlessly, rocking against him and sinking her fingers into his shoulders to draw herself impossibly closer. With another groan that sounded half-hungry, half-pained, he clamped his hands on her hips to hold her still.

But one of his hands began to drift upward, straying into the curve of her waist and higher to the swell of her breast. She arched eagerly into his palm, aching for his touch.

When his hand closed over her breast, they both sucked in a hard breath. Her nipples were already pebbled beneath her gown. At the slide of his thumb over the wool, she practically jumped out of her skin.

But he held her together with his strong arms, his mouth fused to hers and his thumb moving in torturously delicious circles against her nipple.

Sensation was building so fast that Caroline's head spun. A pulse of need thrummed between her legs, insistent, mounting. She squirmed again in his lap, craving so much more. She wanted to feel his bare skin against hers, his mouth on her breasts, his cock driving into her, filling her.

"Touch me," she panted, breaking their kiss. "God, Callum, please."

He sucked in a breath, his arms going stiff around her. "Bloody hell."

His features contorted with frustration, he lifted her from his lap and set her away on the plaid.

He might as well have dumped a bucket of ice water over her head. *What the hell?*

"What are you doing?"

"Stopping this before I cannae anymore."

She stared at him in confusion, her chest rising and falling rapidly. "But why?"

"Honor demands it."

As the haze of lust began to retreat from her mind, his words sank in. A realization clicked into place. This was 1394. People killed and died over honor and virtue —and a woman's virginity.

Caroline let out a shaky breath, relief washing her. "Um, you don't have to worry about my honor, Callum. Things are different in my time. Women have a lot more freedoms. So we can keep going without doing any damage to my reputation."

He leveled her with liquid gold eyes that burned with feral hunger. Wolf's eyes. "*Dinnae*," he practically growled. "Dinnae say things like that, else I'll forget myself again."

"But I'm not a—"

Callum jerked to his feet, giving her his back as he stomped several paces away. He put a hand out to lean against a tree trunk, and his fingers curled into the bark like claws for a long moment. At last, he seemed to regain control of himself, though his breathing was still ragged when he turned back to her.

"It isnae just yer honor I must mind," he said, his voice low and tight. "My duty cannae stray from my clan."

Her brows knit. "What do your responsibilities as Laird have to do with this?"

Muttering something that sounded like a curse, he dragged a hand through his dark hair.

"Forgive me," he said at last, meeting her eyes.

"I told you before, there's nothing to forgive. If you couldn't tell, I wanted that." She waved at the plaid where he'd been embracing her a moment before.

A muscle in his jaw began to dance. "It willnae happen again."

She rose to her feet, planting her hands on her hips. Who knew medieval Highlanders could play mind games with the best of them? "Fine, but I don't understand. I'm not asking for anything from you. This isn't a trap or a ploy. I want you. I thought you wanted me, too." She dragged in a fortifying breath. She couldn't forget her true aim. "I only wanted to see what this could be—until I find a way home, that is."

He seemed to latch on to her last words. "Since ye plan on leaving so soon, it is best no' to muddle things between us. I made ye a promise to keep ye safe until—"

"Until I prove to you that I'm from the future," she cut in.

"Aye, until that time," he said through gritted teeth. "And then I'll take ye to Leannan Falls myself."

"But you said you believe you're just as likely to see pigs fly as accept what I've told you about King James's birth. So which is it? Are you pushing me away because you actually believe I'll be gone soon? Or do you think I'm just some crazy loon who'll be stuck at your castle forever?"

"I dinnae ken," he rasped. "I dinnae ken aught— what to think of ye, what to do with ye, and what to make of my feelings for ye."

Oh. She stood in stunned silence, staring at him.

"Only a fool would try to deny what lies between us," he said, his voice low and soft now. "I have never been drawn to a woman the way I am drawn to ye, Caroline. And that kiss—"

He cut off with a noise that sounded like a strangled curse. "But aught surrounding us is a damned hornets' nest. Ye say ye dinnae belong here, that ye must leave to find yer sisters. But this is my *home*. My people are counting on me to bring peace, to do what is necessary for the betterment of the clan."

A shadow crossed his face, and he worked his jaw for a long moment. Fleetingly, she wondered if more lay beneath his words than she knew, but he went on before she could contemplate that possibility further.

"I dinnae ken what could grow between us if circum- stances were different, but they arenae. And when it comes to kissing ye, touching ye…" He sucked in a ragged breath. "I dinnae trust myself to be able to stop. This could never be just a dalliance, Caroline, or naught more than a trifle. I would always want more. So it is better to halt things now before I cannae halt them anymore."

Caroline swallowed hard. Her stomach swirled with a maelstrom of emotion. He felt it too—the undeniable pull between them, the desire burning hot, the longing for so much more.

And the knowledge that nothing could ever come of this. Not if she had even a sliver of hope to return to her sisters and her own time.

Fresh tears pricked at the back of her eyes, but she blinked them away fiercely.

She didn't want to cry anymore, but what kind of cruel trick was fate playing on her? Why had she been thrown into this time and place, right into Callum's path, only to learn that whatever crazy connection drew them together could never grow into more?

She wanted to scream in frustration, to say to hell with everything, to go to Callum and lose herself in his arms, his hands, his lips again. But doing so would mean throwing away her hope of finding her sisters.

No, she wouldn't turn her back on her family ever again. Even if that meant forsaking her budding feelings for Callum. Relinquishing a place in his life, his home, his time. *His heart.*

"You're right," she said at last, the words barely making it through the tightness in her throat. "It would be best if we put a stop to this before it turns into something that could…distract us from our responsibilities."

He nodded, then moved past her to clear away their little picnic in silence. She stood gazing at the two rings of standing stones while he readied the horse for their departure.

Callum had said the stones always helped him sort through a problem. In a way, they'd worked. Caroline knew what she needed to do—set aside her feelings and stay focused on finding her family. Simple.

But as they rode back toward the castle, chasing the last rays of sunlight, she couldn't help wondering—if things were really so simple, why did it feel like her heart was being torn in two?

EAGAN STOOD ON THE BATTLEMENTS, squinting into the rapidly falling dusk.

The Laird should have been back to the castle well before now. Bron and the others had ridden through the gates hours ago, reassuring Eagan that the Laird was taking Caroline Sutton to the standing stones and had specifically instructed them to return without him.

But Callum had said they would be back before the evening meal, which had already come and gone. With night drawing closer, Eagan feared something had gone terribly wrong. Mayhap the Laird's horse had been lamed. Or mayhap a band of audacious MacBeans had strayed well past the border.

Or mayhap that woman had gotten up to something.

Eagan resisted the urge to spit in disgust over the edge of the curtain wall. He was the seneschal to the

Lairds of Kinmuir Castle, not some crude farmer or mercenary.

Still, it did not take a seneschal's sharp attention and knowledge of all that went on in his keep to see what was happening.

Caroline Sutton was casting some sort of spell over all those in the castle—and most especially the Laird.

Whether it was true black magic or merely a fascination with her odd ways and the allure of her feminine wiles, Eagan didn't care. It wasn't his place to know the difference—only to protect the castle, his Laird, and his clan.

And the lass was threatening all three.

The Laird was clearly taken with her. Eagan had seen them nigh kissing in the garden a sennight past, and watched from the keep as the Laird had ridden off with the lass in his lap that morn.

If Callum continued to forget his place, his responsibility, the whole clan would suffer. Their alliance with the MacConnells would fall through, and the peace Callum's father Duncan had fought so tirelessly for would be squandered.

And if the MacBeans were truly bold enough, they would break not only their border, but might even try to claim Kinmuir as well. Though MacMorans had held this castle for several generations, one weak link in the chain could destroy all that. That was the way of things in the Highlands. Any sign of vulnerability, and the wolves descended.

Worry knotting his stomach, Eagan turned to one of the guards on the wall, preparing to give the order to organize a search party for the Laird. But just as he began to speak, Callum's distinct whistle cut through the gloaming.

A guard farther down the wall sent an answering whistle, and several men began ratcheting up the portcullis. Eagan scanned the twilit moors again, his gaze fastening on a horse trotting toward the castle.

He breathed a sigh of relief when he picked out Callum's dark form atop the horse, then frowned at the sight of the woman still sitting in the Laird's lap.

Eagan hurried down from the wall. He'd just reached the yard when the gates swung open and Callum rode in. From the stiff way the Laird dismounted and lifted Caroline down, he hadn't completely gone daft over her, thank God. Still, despite the falling darkness, Eagan didn't miss the look that passed between them and the way the Laird's hands lingered on her waist before he snatched them away.

"Laird," Eagan said, clasping his hands behind his back. "I was just about to send a party to look for ye."

Callum handed his reins to one of the lads who'd come running from the stables. "No need," he replied brusquely.

Eagan opened his mouth to remind the Laird in the firmest terms short of crossing into disrespect that it wasn't wise to ride after dusk with MacBeans growing more savage by the day—and the MacConnell alliance hanging in the balance—but Callum brushed by him, striding stonily toward the keep.

Caroline followed, though she walked much slower. As the Laird yanked open the keep's double doors, light from the great hall spilled out into the yard, casting Caroline in a yellow glow.

A glow that clearly revealed lips that were swollen and red—from kissing the Laird no doubt.

Eagan swallowed hard. It was worse than he'd thought. He stood rooted for a long moment, until both the Laird and the lass had entered the keep and the doors had closed behind them. Inside, his mind churned.

As seneschal, it was his duty to ensure the smooth running of the castle. But more than that, he'd served the MacMoran Lairds, Callum and Duncan before him, for more than three decades. If Callum couldn't see the danger he was in—the danger he was putting them *all* in —Eagan had to find a way to show him.

An idea taking hold, he hurried into the great hall. But he didn't slow once he was inside. Instead, he strode to the west tower stairs. As he climbed toward the solar, he began composing a missive in his head.

Chapter Fourteen

A t last the rains had come. The day after Callum and Caroline had visited the stones, the wind had whipped up and the skies had turned tumultuous. In the sennight since then, storm after storm had blown through.

Some were hardly more than a gentle caress, as if the clouds were reaching down to brush against the hills and moors, leaving them lightly misted and damp. Other storms seemed to attempt to pummel the land into submission with lashing downpours and howling winds.

Today was one of the latter. Callum didn't mind, though. It suited his mood.

He stood in the yard before a dozen of his men, running them through drill after drill. Most hunched into their plaids, water sluicing from their beards, practice swords slipping from their numb hands.

Callum, on the other hand, stood only in his tunic,

trews, and boots. He wanted to *feel* the pelt of the rain, the biting wind, the ache in his muscles as he moved through another sequence of sword maneuvers—anything besides the throbbing in his chest.

He willed himself not to glance at the topmost chamber in the east tower. The rains had driven Caroline away from her garden, and she'd spent much of her time in her chamber.

It was better this way. A few days past, when the downpour had let up to little more than a gentle mist, she'd checked on her plants and collected a few vegetables and pears for Tilly. Callum had strained so hard to catch a glimpse of her around the edge of the keep that he'd nearly taken a blow to the head from Bron's wooden practice sword.

Aye, it was better now that he only saw her briefly for meals. Never mind the fact that she filled his mind at every other waking moment—and haunted his dreams as well.

And here he was thinking of her—her eyes like blue fire, her lips, her scent—yet again.

"I've never seen so many Highland warriors enfeebled by a wee bit of rain," he barked at his men. "Taggard, if that sword slips from yer grip one more time, I'll tie it to yer hands. Hamish, quit huddling under yer plaid like an auld woman and square yer shoulders against yer opponent. We willnae stop until every last one of ye—"

Behind him, the portcullis groaned and the gates creaked open.

"What the bloody hell?" he muttered, tossing aside

his practice sword and stomping through the mud and puddled water toward the slowly opening gates.

Suddenly a lad on horseback shot through the slim gap in the gates, clumps of mud flying behind him. He reined in hard, sending another spray of mud around him.

"Who the hell are ye?" Callum snapped, holding up a hand against the rain of muddy water. "And what in God's name are ye doing riding into my castle in this manner?"

It wasn't until the mud had stopped flying that Callum realized the lad wore the patch of a messenger on the sleeve of his tunic. The lad, who couldn't have been more than seventeen, was breathing nearly as heavily as his horse. His cheeks were flushed red, either from his hard riding or the cool weather, or both. Yet he hopped down from his horse with surprising agility and gave Callum a quick bow.

"Laird MacMoran?"

"Aye," he replied warily.

The lad dug into the pouch on his waist, removing a small packet wrapped in waxed parchment. As he handed the packet to Callum, he grinned from ear to ear.

"I was tasked with delivering the news ye requested, Laird. Yer missive made it clear that ye wished to be informed with all haste about the birth of the King and Queen's bairn. I've ridden straight from Dunfermline Abbey in only three days." He lifted his chin proudly. "A journey that takes most messengers five."

Over the sudden thunder of blood filling his ears,

Callum distantly realized that the lad should be compensated for his extra efforts at promptness.

"Come inside and warm yerself, lad," he murmured, staring at the packet in his hand. "Eat yer fill. Yer horse will be looked after as well."

"Thank ye, Laird," the lad said with another wide grin before darting off to the keep. Callum followed, but his feet moved far slower than the boy's.

Good God. He hadn't expected word of the Queen's birth to arrive so quickly. The messenger had said it had taken him three days to ride from Dunfermline, which meant…After making the quick calculation in his head, Callum cursed. If the lad had left straightaway, which he likely had given his eagerness to deliver his news speedily, that would put the birth on the twenty-fifth of July.

Just what Caroline had predicted.

Nay, not *predicted*. If he was to believe what she claimed, she hadn't guessed at the future. She *knew* it, because the events had already happened in her time.

It was only one detail, he reminded himself. Everyone knew the Queen carried another bairn. There were only so many days she might deliver to choose from.

Still, his pace quickened as he entered the great hall and strode toward the east tower stairs. He held the answers to all the odd riddles about Caroline—her abrupt and unexplained appearance at Loch Darraig, her strange accent, her peculiar words and tales—folded in his hands. It seemed only fitting to settle this with her.

Before he realized it, he stood in front of her door. He knocked once, and at her beckon, he stepped inside.

She sat on the large chest, which she'd pulled beneath her window. She turned from gazing down at the garden, starting slightly at the sight of him. Her lips parted to speak, but he held up the folded parchment.

"A missive with news from Dunfermline has arrived."

She stilled, yet to his surprise, she seemed more resigned than anxious, as if she already knew what he'd find inside the missive. Aye, well, that was exactly what she claimed to know.

He removed the protective wax wrapping and quickly unfolded the parchment inside. He scanned the words scratched in ink, his pulse thudding in his ears. Then he read them again.

He had to swallow against a suddenly dry throat.

"It is," he began, pausing to clear his throat. "It is as ye said. The Queen was safely delivered of a bairn on the twenty-fifth of July. A boy, to be known as James."

When he lowered the parchment, she was gazing at him, her features unreadable.

"Do you believe me now?"

His last rational defenses made one final stand. But as he ran through each in his mind, they fell away. It might be chance or luck to guess the date correctly. And the bairn's sex was an even chance, like the flip of a coin. Yet how had she known they would name him James?

As far as Callum knew, James wasn't a family name for either the King or the Queen. The name Robert was, of course, but they'd given their first-born son that moniker. And to their second they gave the name

David. John was the Queen's father's name, and Robert III's name before he'd taken the crown. But no Jameses came to mind on either side of the royal family tree.

"I…I dinnae ken what to think."

But a voice whispered in the back of his head that he *did* know. Mayhap he'd known all along. He'd thought her daft at first, but never that she was lying. She'd been steadfast in insisting that she was…from the future. Even now, his mind lurched over the very idea.

Yet it would explain so much. Her lucid descriptions of strange lands and peoples, their ways and habits as natural and familiar to her as his were to him. The revealing garments she'd arrived in, unlike aught he'd ever seen.

And her insistence that she find a way to return home. How well would Callum have fared if he'd arrived in *her* time? The idea was so hard to grasp that it made his head spin.

"How…how can this be true?" He glanced down at the parchment, then back at Caroline. "How can ye have fallen back…how long did ye say?"

"More than six hundred years," she breathed. "And I don't know."

She stood from the chest and walked slowly to her bed, sitting and crossing her legs under her. As if he were sleepwalking, Callum followed, lowering himself onto the edge of the bed opposite her.

"I don't understand any of it," she went on. "Like I told you, I was in the present—my present—and my sisters and I jumped from the top of Leannan Falls. All of a sudden they were gone, and I was spinning like crazy, and then I popped up in Loch Darraig."

"And ye dinnae have the faintest idea how it happened?"

"No," she replied. "The loch doesn't seem to have anything to do with it, though. Leannan Falls might be the key—or maybe I opened some wormhole or vortex or something and the falls isn't the answer either. But I at least have to return to the falls. It's my best chance of getting home."

When her eyes met his, they were clouded with a tempest of emotion to rival the storm outside.

"Will you keep your promise to take me there?"

Her words were like a punch to the gut. He'd made that pledge never thinking to have to keep it. But he was still a man of his word—a man of honor.

"Aye," he said, his voice low and tight in his throat. "It is too late in the day to depart now, but come tomorrow, we will set out for the falls. Rain or shine."

This would be it, then. Her last night under his roof. They would have nearly a sennight's worth of travel to reach the falls, but then she would be gone from his life.

He wanted to curse whatever magic or spirit or demon had brought her to him, only to draw her away so soon. But the truth was, he was no longer sure any length of time with Caroline would be enough.

Except forever.

He instantly quashed the thought and the emotion that rose with them. She'd made it abundantly clear that she wanted to return to her sisters and her own time more than aught that remained here for her.

A heavy silence fell over them, broken only by the drone of the rain outside. He nearly stood to leave, steeling himself with a few terse words about being ready for their journey tomorrow, but then he stopped himself.

If he could trade his pride to spend a few more hours at his mother's bedside, or share another dram of whisky with his father, he would. But they were both gone. His time with them had been fleeting, just as it was with Caroline. Yet she still sat before him, flesh and blood, warmth and light.

"Would ye..." He cleared the tightness from his throat. "Would ye tell me something of yer time?"

Her dark brows shot up. "Really?"

"Aye."

She gnawed on her lower lip for a moment. "What do you want to know?"

Callum leaned back against one of the bed's posters, drinking in the sight of her across from him, so bonny and bold. His wee enchantress. His heart.

"Anything. Everything."

Chapter Fifteen

Caroline stifled a yawn with the back of her hand. It was the first time in nearly three weeks of living in 1394 that she truly missed coffee.

She and Callum had stayed up almost the entire night talking. He'd been endlessly curious—if at times disbelieving—about the strange picture she painted of the future.

She'd been careful to consider what she told him, lest she unintentionally change the course of history. But she saw no harm in describing airplanes, indoor plumbing, modern medicine, and computers, though she'd struggled with the last a bit since in truth, she didn't really understand them herself. She'd spoken of the ever-shifting powers of politics, and even the fact that a new continent, her future homeland, would be discovered across a vast ocean in a hundred years or so.

When at last the sky had begun to lighten with the

first blush of dawn, he'd left, urging her to get at least a few winks of sleep. They had a big day ahead of them.

Judging from the cheery sunlight streaming in through her window, it was mid-morning now. But instead of feeling excited to finally be setting off for Leannan Falls, sadness sat like a stone in her stomach.

She was leaving.

She'd kept herself busy for a few minutes that morning by dressing and gathering a couple of extra gowns and chemises, as well as her old clothes, for the journey. But once she'd packed them into a leather satchel, she had nothing else to do. The sparse little chamber seemed to stare back at her, wondering what she was still doing there.

Straightening her spine, she grabbed the satchel and descended the stairs to the great hall. Breakfast had already been served and cleared away, so the hall was empty and quiet as she crossed to the double doors. The yard outside, however, bustled with activity.

A half dozen MacMoran warriors stood around their mounts, tightening buckles and adjusting straps on saddlebags. Callum stood in the center, holding the reins of a dappled gray horse that looked more like a pony compared to the men's giant steeds.

He'd promised to pick out the most docile, sweet-tempered mare for her. Caroline had asked for the oldest, most pacified horse, but Callum had insisted that although she would need a tame mount, inexperienced horsewoman that she was, the animal had to be spry enough to make the week-long journey ahead of them.

Though she longed to go straight to Callum, she

wanted to say goodbye to the garden first. She slipped around the edge of the keep and through the wooden gate, leaning against the stone wall for a moment to gaze upon the little patch of heaven.

Despite several brutal downpours, the plants seemed to be thriving. Everything glistened with yesterday's rain in the morning sun, making each leaf and flower look like a jewel.

Oh, she would miss this place—the castle and the sprawling wilderness surrounding it, yes, but most of all this tiny corner of wild, chaotic, overgrown life. Unable to help herself, she plucked one last errant weed before letting a breath go and turning to join Callum.

But just outside the garden's walls, Tilly stood waiting, Margaret right behind her.

"Safe travels, mistress," Tilly said, wringing her hands in the folds of her apron. "I packed enough food for over a fortnight, but dinnae let the men take more than their share. We cannae send ye home hungry."

Tilly patted Caroline's arm lightly, but then she made one of those Scottish noises of frustration in the back of her throat and abruptly pulled Caroline into a snug embrace. "Thank ye, lass. I'll do my best to keep up the garden. I willnae let it get into such a bad state again, I vow."

"I'll help Ma, as well," Margaret said, giving Caroline a soft smile over her mother's shoulder. "We all do so appreciate yer hard work, mistress."

Caroline found that her throat was suddenly too pinched to do more than murmur her thanks to both women.

When Tilly released her at last and stepped back, dabbing at her hazel eyes, Caroline's gaze landed on Eagan, who stood back from the others in the yard, observing. His hands were clasped behind his back, and though his features were bland as ever, she noticed the faintest curve to his lips behind his neatly-trimmed beard.

The seneschal had never warmed to her, but that wasn't her problem anymore.

"Bye, Eagan," she said, giving him a nod but not slowing as she made her way toward the waiting men.

"Safe travels, mistress," he said evenly.

When she reached Callum, she let herself drink in the sight of him. Now that the rains had been chased away and the sun shone cheerily overhead, his hair glinted like polished mahogany. He'd tied it back at the base of his strong neck for the journey.

The hard lines of his jaw were smooth and firm, his mouth set in a neutral line. But when she met his eyes, they revealed a flicker of the emotion he hid behind his impassive features. Their honey depths warmed on her, then tightened with sadness.

"Ready?" he murmured.

She drew in a shaking breath. "Y—"

"A band of riders approaches, Laird!" one of the guards called from the wall.

"What?" Callum muttered, frowning up at the guard.

"They bear MacConnell colors."

"Let them in."

As the portcullis was lifted and the gates opened,

Callum handed the mare's reins to a stable lad and strode from the group of men to face whoever had just arrived. Unsure of what to do, Caroline hung back, peering around horses and the warriors' shoulders to see what was going on.

Even before the gates were fully open, a dozen mounted men wearing blue and brown plaids rode into the yard. At their front was a broad-shouldered, barrel-chested man of perhaps fifty, his graying brown hair whipped into a frenzy around his head from his ride. His bright blue eyes blazed with anger.

"Laird MacConnell, welcome," Callum said levelly, though Caroline didn't miss the note of surprise in his voice. "What brings ye to Kinmuir so unexpect—"

The man's bushy eyebrows winged at Callum's use of English, but he followed suit without question when he cut in. "I had to see for myself if the missive I received was true," he said, his sharp words booming over the yard. He swept keen eyes over those gathered. When his gaze fixed on Caroline, his brows shot up again.

"So it is true, then."

"What is true?" Callum said, some of his composure slipping. "And what missive are ye speaking of?"

"I received word a few days past that ye've been harboring a strange woman under yer roof," Laird MacConnell said, pinning Callum with a withering look. "The missive encouraged me to remind ye of our arrangement—the arrangement yer *father* believed was best for both our clans."

MacConnell's piercing gaze flickered to Caroline

before returning to Callum. "I would have yer word, here and now, MacMoran, that ye havenae reneged on our agreement."

He motioned over his shoulder at his men, who began moving aside. Caroline rose on her toes to try to see what was happening. As the MacConnell men parted, she realized there was another rider on a smaller mount in their midst. *A woman.*

"Well, MacMoran?" Laird MacConnell demanded. "Will ye keep yer vow and marry my daughter?"

Chapter Sixteen

✿❀✿

C allum was *engaged*?

Caroline took a step back so abruptly that she bumped into one of the MacMoran warriors. Heat climbed into her face and her throat squeezed as if someone had clamped a hand around it.

He turned to her and their gazes collided. Those amber wolf eyes pinned her, trying to communicate... something, but Caroline couldn't tell what through the storm of confusion breaking over her. All she could do was stand there gaping like a fish.

How could he not have mentioned that he was engaged? How could he have kissed her like that—like a man dying of thirst, and she was the first sip of water he'd had in ages. And how could he have said all those things about wanting more with her, of not being able to stop himself?

Honor demands it. His words drifted back through the

maelstrom in her mind. *It isnae just yer honor I must mind. My duty cannae stray from my clan.*

Of course. His duty to his clan—to marry Laird MacConnell's daughter and forge the alliance he so desperately needed. In his oblique way, he'd been talking about *his* honor—or maybe the honor of the young woman sitting atop her horse in the middle of the yard.

Caroline truly looked at her for the first time.

She couldn't have been more than eighteen, her skin a flawless combination of peaches and cream. Her hair shone in the sun like spun gold. She cast wide blue eyes, the same vibrant color as her father's, around all those gathered in the yard, a demure blush rising to her cheeks. Even seated in her saddle, Caroline could tell the woman was both petite of build and lushly curvaceous.

A sudden stab of jealousy lanced through Caroline's gut. *Yes.* This was the woman Callum would marry. Pretty. Perfect. A woman of his own world.

She wasn't normally one to become petty when it came to other women. Raised with her family's unconditional love and the belief that a woman's appearance meant little compared to her character, she rarely compared herself to others and instead aimed focus on her own goals and accomplishments.

But standing there in a drab green wool gown for traveling, her brown hair pulled back into a simple braid, Caroline felt plain. More than that, she felt *excluded*. It was as if her life had suddenly become a movie starring other people. She'd had her heart set on getting the hell out of this era since she'd arrived. But for the first time, it truly struck her that life here would go on without her. *Callum's* life would go on without her.

That realization made it feel as though her heart was being squeezed by a garbage compactor.

Callum had squared himself to Laird MacConnell once more, crossing his arms over his chest.

"Who sent ye this missive?" he demanded.

"It doesnae matter," Laird MacConnell countered. "For now that I see its contents are true, I'll have answers from ye. I ask ye again, MacMoran, will ye see this alliance through, or will ye break yer word and go against Duncan's wishes?"

"I'd kindly request that ye dinnae throw my father's name at me in my own damn castle," Callum growled. "Ye'll have answers from me soon enough, but at least give me the courtesy of an explanation as to what the bloody hell is going on."

Callum's harsh tone made Laird MacConnell draw back slightly. His horse shifted beneath him, and he took a moment to soothe the animal and gather his words.

"In truth, I dinnae ken who sent the missive," MacConnell replied, somewhat calmer now. "As I said, it arrived a few days past. I didnae think it wise to wait on the matter, so I gathered my men and Aileas straightaway to ride here and see for myself."

"MacBean," Callum muttered through clenched teeth. "He kenned of Caroline's presence at Kinmuir. And he stands to gain the most from inciting discord between us. He kens that once we are allied, reining him in will be our joint aim. No wonder he sought to sow conflict."

"The fact is, it doesnae matter who sent it," MacConnell replied tightly. "Ye dinnae deny that ye've been harboring that woman—Caroline." He pointed right at her. "And nor have ye denied that her presence endangers our alliance."

For the first time, MacConnell seemed to notice the fact that several MacMorans stood behind their Laird, mounts at the ready. "Am I to believe, too, that I have come upon ye in the midst of absconding with her, MacMoran?"

This was all too much. Was MacConnell implying that Caroline was some sort of...*whore*? And that Callum was running away with her?

Apparently, the implication didn't miss Callum, either.

"Caroline Sutton is a woman of *honor*," he ground out. "She is under my protection from the MacBeans. Breathe another word against her and face my sword." He drew in a lungful of air, visibly fighting for composure. "And aye, I was about to escort her to..." He searched for the right words for a moment. "To the Lowlands, so that she may continue her journey home safely."

Laird MacConnell narrowed his eyes on Callum. "Ye arenae going anywhere until we sort this matter out, MacMoran. I dinnae take kindly to even the faintest whiff of unseemliness when it comes to this alliance. The lass will just have to wait."

"No!" Caroline blurted, finding her voice for the first time since Laird MacConnell's abrupt arrival. As several dozen sets of eyes shifted to her, she swallowed hard but held her chin steady. She found Callum's gaze. "You promised to take me, Callum."

"Forgive me," he murmured.

Oh, no. This time there *was* something to forgive, but Caroline wasn't giving up so easily. "You *promised*," she repeated, her voice low and strained.

Suddenly Eagan had joined the fray. His calm, vaguely smug look from earlier had vanished, to be replaced with deep creases of worry. "Surely ye can send the lass on her own, Laird. She neednae interrupt yer talks with Laird MacConnell."

"Nay," Callum ground out. "Girolt MacBean is still out there, hoping for the chance to use her against me. I willnae give him such an opportunity."

Eagan clasped his hands in front of him so tightly that his knuckles blanched. "Then send a contingent of warriors with her." He nodded toward the MacMoran men, who stood tensed and waiting for an order from their Laird. "Surely that satisfies yer need to guarantee the lass's wellbeing."

"Nay," Callum said again. His eyes flickered to her, hard as crystalized chips of amber. "*I* took responsibility for Caroline's protection, and *I* vowed to see her safely to the Lowlands. I gave my word, and I intend to keep it."

He glanced meaningfully at Laird MacConnell at that, then his gaze fixed on Caroline once more. His eyes softened ever so slightly in a silent plea. "In time, I will take ye where ye wish to go, Caroline."

In time? It had already been nearly three weeks since she'd tumbled through the falls and into Callum's world.

Her sisters were no doubt beside themselves with worry. They'd already lost so much. They couldn't lose each other now, too.

Hot tears of anger pricking her eyes, she opened her mouth to tell him as much, but Eagan spoke first.

"But Laird, there must be a way to——"

"Enough," Callum snapped. "Eagan, prepare chambers for our guests. Tilly——" His gaze shifted to the cook, who stood huddled and wide-eyed against the keep's doors. "——See that refreshments are made ready. Come, Laird MacConnell." He fixed the man with a flinty stare. "I believe we have much to discuss."

Chapter Seventeen

As Callum stalked into the great hall, he silently bellowed every foul curse he knew.

Damn it all.

Damn Laird MacConnell for arriving at Kinmuir—with his daughter Aileas, no less—puffing himself up as if he were ready to go to war.

Damn Girolt MacBean for meddling in the MacMorans' alliance with the MacConnells.

And damn himself for breaking his word to Caroline. The look she'd given him—disappointment and hurt and sadness and anger, all distilled into her ice-blue eyes—had been like a dagger in his chest.

He would still take her to Leannan Falls, he vowed. But until MacConnell could be diverted off the war path, that would have to wait.

Callum halted just inside the keep's doors, Laird MacConnell close on his heels.

"Tell yer men to wait in the yard," he ordered flatly.

MacConnell narrowed those sharp blue eyes at him. "Why? So ye can corner me in here with the rest of yer MacMorans and—"

"We are civilized men," Callum cut in. "We have broken bread many a time in this hall. And as ye've reminded me more than once this morn, my father sought an alliance between our clans. I willnae be the first to strike against ye. If *ye* wish to attack me, however, by all means, bring yer warriors in."

MacConnell frowned, but after a moment, he gave the order to his men to wait outside.

Callum strode to the table on the raised dais, taking up his chair and pointing to the one across from him.

"This concerns my daughter, too," MacConnell said. "She'll hear what ye have to say as well, MacMoran."

Aileas lingered behind her father, looking around uncertainly. MacConnell shoved out a chair beside himself, and the lass hesitantly lowered into it.

"Verra well," Callum growled. "But Caroline stays, too. I willnae have her maligned behind her back—or before it, for that matter."

Caroline had been about to slip up the east tower stairs, but she froze, one foot lifted on the first step. "I don't need to—"

"Come." His tone brooked no argument. He gestured toward a chair next to him.

Reluctantly, she walked to the dais and took the chair he'd indicated.

He was afforded a few more moments to gather his thoughts when Tilly hurried from the swinging kitchen door, carrying a tray loaded with bread, cheese, butter, and honey. She also carried a pitcher of ale and several cups.

"Ye must be weary from yer journey," Callum said, aiming for a calm air.

Laird MacConnell bluntly tore a hunk of bread from the loaf Tilly had brought, shoving a piece in his mouth. But judging from the way his eyes glittered with distrust, this wasn't a true sign of warming between them. He was satisfying the traditions of hospitality, naught more.

The ritual of breaking bread complete, MacConnell openly glared at Callum.

"Will ye answer me now, MacMoran? Will our alliance move forward, or have...distractions caused ye to lose yer way?" His gaze darted to Caroline before settling on Callum once more.

"I havenae lost aught," Callum replied. "But I would remind ye that I cannae lose what I never had in the first place. My engagement with Aileas was never formalized, Laird, nor have we pledged ourselves in a hand-fasting."

Beside him, Caroline stiffened. He'd wanted to say so much to her out in the yard, but most of all that he hadn't intended to use or mislead her. It was true, a marriage alliance between himself and Aileas had been discussed three years past. But it was also true that no formal arrangement had ever been made.

"Dinnae disrespect me and my daughter by claiming that we didnae have an understanding," MacConnell snarled.

"I dinnae intend any disrespect," Callum countered

evenly. "Only to speak plainly of the truth of the matter."

"It was Duncan's wish before he passed that our clans be united. Are ye saying that ye would go against yer father's hopes for a peaceful alliance?"

Callum's hands clenched beneath the table. "I warned ye once about throwing my father's name at me in my own home. Aye, it was his wish that we ally our clans through marriage. I believe that in the three years since his death, I have shown that I am more than willing to build upon the peace between our peoples. MacMorans and MacConnells alike have stood along our shared border with the MacBeans."

"Aye, they have," MacConnell acknowledged grudgingly. "But ye ken as well as I that it isnae enough anymore, no' when the MacBeans grow bolder by the day. Standing side by side is all well and good. Yet naught binds two clans as well as blood. Marry Aileas, and yer sons would be my grandsons."

"I ken that. But I would remind ye again that no such arrangement was ever made formal between us."

MacConnell pounded a fist on the table, making both Aileas and Caroline jump. "And are ye saying that it *willnae* be formalized?"

Callum let a long breath go. Bloody hell, what a shite-storm this was turning into. MacConnell was making it clear that the only way he would go forward with an alliance was through an arranged marriage between Callum and Aileas.

In truth, Callum couldn't fault him for that. Many an agreement between clans had fallen apart over petty squabbles and misunderstandings. But joining through marriage—and blood—made the bonds far stronger. And far harder to break when the winds of fate and fortune shifted.

But every fiber in him screamed not to bind himself for life to the lass sitting across from him. He let himself look upon Aileas. She was bonny, there was no denying it, yet she didn't stir aught in him. *Not like Caroline.*

And he didn't even know the lass. The last time he'd seen her, she'd been a girl of fifteen, painfully shy and so quiet he hadn't heard her speak a single word throughout the feast Laird MacConnell had hosted.

At that feast, Callum's father had broached the subject of a marriage alliance. Both Duncan and Laird MacConnell had agreed that Aileas was too young. They'd decided that the matter should be taken up more seriously later, but at the time, it had been enough to merely suggest the possibility. That had been the foundation of goodwill between the two clans which Callum had been working to build upon ever since.

As the future Laird, Callum had been raised with the understanding that his marriage would be used for the strategic purposes of an alliance—and his wife would likely be a stranger, a lass who could benefit his clan's position. Naught more.

But everything had changed when Caroline had come crashing into his life. Callum had let himself forget his responsibility. He'd let himself imagine a future with her. A life based on *love*.

He hadn't let himself think the word, for some part of him knew it was a fool's errand to hope for it.

And he'd been right. Laird MacConnell was here to remind him of that—that love must always cede to duty.

Still, some daft, defiant part of him fought to hold out.

"Would ye agree that we have continued to work toward peace between our clans in the years since my father's death?" Callum asked, avoiding MacConnell's demand for a plain answer regarding the marriage alliance.

MacConnell eyed him warily. "Aye."

"That has been enough for the last three years. Why dinnae we table the matter of a formal arrangement, with the understanding that our interests, especially regarding the MacBeans' overreach, continue to align."

To Callum's surprise, Aileas spoke. "Aye, Father, that is wise given—"

MacConnell cut her off. "My daughter is already eighteen! Aye, it made sense to wait when she was just a wee bairn of fifteen, but she is a woman grown now. She ought to be married. There isnae any good reason to delay longer." Once again, the Laird's cold gaze slid to Caroline. "Unless yer loyalties have...*shifted*, MacMoran."

Callum stiffened, but he managed to bite back the harsh reply that rose to his tongue.

The truth was, his loyalties *had* shifted. Three sennights ago, he never would have attempted to delay, or outright abandon, the possibility of marrying Aileas to secure his alliance with the MacConnells.

Yet in that short time, his whole world had been turned upside down. Some inexplicable bond tied him to Caroline. Some invisible force had thrown them together and intertwined their hearts.

And would soon enough tear them apart once more. He prayed that Caroline would forgive him for postponing their journey to Leannan Falls, but whether they left tomorrow or in a sennight or in a year, she still wished to leave.

Still, even if they were fated to remain separated by the centuries, Callum could not go back to the life he'd had before. He could not marry for duty. Not when he'd experienced so much more with Caroline. But would that mean he'd destroy his clan's chance for peace, all in the name of love?

Suddenly, his shoulders felt weighted with a lifetime of burdens. He pinched the bridge of his nose, letting a long breath go.

"It seems we are at an impasse for the time being, Laird MacConnell," he murmured. "Mayhap ye and yer daughter ought to rest after yer journey, and we can resume this discussion when we are all refreshed."

Laird MacConnell pushed back from the table. "We can rest and break bread and drink ale and talk all ye like, MacMoran. But it willnae change my mind. The only question that remains is when will my patience run out?"

Chapter Eighteen

Caroline rolled over for what felt like the hundredth time that night. The keep was quiet. The shutter was closed against the silvery light of the moon. The embers burned low in the brazier, providing cozy warmth.

Nothing was amiss.

Except *everything* was amiss.

She stared at the canopy over her bed, replaying every painful moment of the day.

It had been torture to sit in the great hall and listen to all that talk of Callum marrying Aileas. It was just another reminder that Caroline didn't belong here, that her life was incompatible with Callum's—whereas Callum and Aileas were perfectly matched.

Caroline's only consolation was that Callum had seemed to be trying to find a way out of it. Still, that didn't take away the sting of being blindsided by the knowledge that he was going to marry another.

Even though the engagement wasn't official, he should have told her, she thought heatedly. She never would have kissed him or let herself fantasize about what it could be like between them if she'd known.

Guilt chewed the edge off her anger at that thought. Hadn't she been the one to declare that there could be no future for them? To insist that she was leaving as soon as possible?

Her own words from a week past, so cavalierly spoken, came back to her. *I'm not asking for anything from you.* She winced at that. *I only want to see what this could be —until I find a way home, that is.*

She'd imagined that she could indulge her lust, her curiosity, with no strings attached. The problem was, there *were* strings attached now—and one string in particular that seemed to bind her heart to his.

And judging from the way he'd attempted that morning to calm Laird MacConnell and find an alternative that didn't involve marrying Aileas, maybe he felt the same. But even if he didn't, who was she to be mad at him? She'd made it abundantly clear that she wanted to get back to her own time and find her sisters.

It fanned her anger once more to think of how he'd broken his promise to take her to Leannan Falls. Sure, he'd said he would take her *in time*, and maybe he would, but it made her want to scream in helpless frustration to be forced to wait when she might only be a week's journey from reuniting with her sisters.

Luckily, Laird MacConnell had declined a lavish meal that evening, declaring instead that he and his daughter would rest in their chambers until tomorrow.

That had meant Caroline had been spared the misery of having to sit in the great hall and listen to more back-and-forth about Callum marrying Aileas. But it had also meant that she hadn't seen or spoken to Callum since that morning.

It was for the best, she told herself as she lay in a tangle of blankets, fighting back the tears that had threatened all day. What else did they have to say to each other? Nothing had changed, except for a brief delay in their departure for the falls. She was still leaving for her own world. And he was staying here in his.

The thought should have comforted her, but it only made her stomach swirl and her chest squeeze painfully. With a frustrated breath, she threw the covers back and rose. Though it was probably well past midnight, she longed for the peace and calm of the garden.

She dressed hurriedly, slinging a cloak around her shoulders to keep the nighttime chill at bay. When she slipped out of her chamber, she listened for a long moment, but the keep was quiet and still.

She padded down the stairs, her slippers silent. But when she reached the landing below hers, she froze.

Callum's door stood solidly closed before her.

She thought for a long moment about knocking softly, turning the knob, and gliding inside. His clean, intoxicating scent would surround her as she tucked herself into his warm bed. She'd find him there, hard and hot and so hungry for her that he would tear through her clothes and drive himself between her spread thighs.

No. She drew back, exhaling raggedly. What would

going to him now change? Nothing. It would only break her heart more, knowing what she couldn't have.

Forcing her feet to move, she continued down the stairs until she reached the great hall. Embers in each of the giant hearths cast a faint orange glow over the hall, just enough to make out the sleeping forms of the men covering the ground.

The hall was more crowded than usual, what with Laird MacConnell's men joining the MacMorans to sleep on pallets or wrapped in their plaids. Despite the tighter than normal quarters, they all slept soundly. Several snores drifted through the otherwise quiet space.

Caroline picked her way between the sleeping warriors, careful not to step on them or even brush them with her skirts lest she disturb them. When she reached the keep's doors, she cracked one open and squeezed through, closing it silently behind her.

Drawing her cloak tighter against the cool night, she hurried toward the garden. Only when she'd slipped through the gate did the knots in her stomach begin to loosen.

A brief, soft rain had fallen earlier in the evening, but a gentle breeze had chased away the clouds, leaving the nearly full moon and stars bare in the dark, clear sky. Caroline let their silvered light wash over her. She couldn't remember the last time she'd seen so many stars.

She drew in a deep breath of sweet, fresh air. Everything smelled damp and alive and growing. In the glow of the moonlight, the garden looked wilder, less orderly. Lush green life tumbled out of the raised beds and climbed the keep's side, squeezing against the stones walling the garden in.

It should have made Caroline feel better. Should have given her strength and peace, as being in nature normally did. Instead, all the abundant, verdant growth around her only stood in contrast to the withering heart inside her chest.

Her back bumped into the garden wall, and she slid down until she was crouched on the rich, dark soil. At last, the tears that she'd been fighting all day broke free.

She wept for her sisters, for the part of her that was missing without her family.

She wept for Callum, for the aching, unexpected love that had blossomed when she'd least wanted it, and for the future he would have—without her.

And she wept for herself, torn apart by two different times, two different lives, two different loves.

"Mistress Caroline."

Caroline sucked in a breath and jerked to her feet, dashing her palms over her tear-streaked cheeks.

"Eagan," she breathed, her gaze landing on the seneschal. He stood in the garden's entrance, half of his features lit by the moon and the other half cast in shadow. "What are you doing here?"

"I noticed ye leaving the keep."

So much for slipping out undetected. "And you followed me?"

"I...I want to help ye."

Disbelief made her brows lower. It was obvious that Eagan had never liked her much. What help could he possibly want to give her now?

"What do you mean?" she asked warily.

Eagan picked his words for a moment. "It didnae seem…fair that the Laird promised to take ye to the Lowlands, only to force ye to remain here while he sorts through matters with Laird MacConnell."

Caroline let out a breath. "Apparently I'll be adhering to *his* schedule for the time being."

"I ken ye want to return home—wherever that is," Eagan went on. "And I think ye should be allowed to."

He reached into the folds of his cloak and pulled out a coiled length of rope. Caroline stared at it, confused.

"Ye could leave on yer own. Now," Eagan murmured, extending the rope toward her.

"What?"

"Havenae ye noticed the way the trees at the back of the garden brush against the outer curtain wall?" he asked. "Fasten the rope to a branch, and the other end around yer waist. Climb the tree to the top of the wall, then lower yerself down the other side by the rope. Ye'd be free."

"But…" Caroline's mind spun with a dozen questions. "But I wouldn't have a horse, and I don't even know how to get to—"

"Go to the village on the other side of the castle. Ye'll be able to buy a horse there."

"With what? I don't have any money."

He reached beneath his cloak once more and withdrew a leather satchel much like the one she'd packed that morning in preparation to leave.

"There is coin in here, and food—all ye'll need to get home."

She stared at the rope and the satchel. "Why are you doing this? I know you don't like me, so why are you trying to help me?"

Eagan lowered the rope and bag, meeting her gaze. His blue-gray eyes looked paler where the moonlight shot through them. "It isnae a matter of whether I like ye or no'. I am trying to protect my clan—and the Laird. Ye are a distraction to him, a diversion from his responsibility."

He waved toward the keep, and she thought of Laird MacConnell and Aileas sleeping inside. And of Callum and his need to secure peace for his people. Tears burned in her eyes.

"I know," she said, her voice tight and low.

"I dinnae ken where ye are from, nor do I care, but ye dinnae belong here. Ye must ken that, too—that is why ye've been trying to leave. Let me help ye."

That was it—he wanted to get rid of her. He wanted to clear the path for Callum to refocus on his duty and marry Aileas. It just so happened that his goal of being rid of Caroline overlapped with hers of getting to Leannan Falls.

It was an uncomfortable alliance, but they could both get what they wanted. And Eagan was right. Caroline didn't belong here—in this century or in Callum's life.

Caroline swallowed hard, straightening her spine. She'd done enough dwelling and crying and overthinking. It was time she took action.

Reaching out, she grabbed the rope and satchel from Eagan's hands.

"Ye are making the right decision," he breathed, giving her a nod. "If ye do as I said and move quickly, the guards willnae notice ye, for they dinnae watch this section of the wall as closely. I must return to the keep. Safe travels."

He turned to slip out of the garden, but she called out softly.

"Wait. Thank you, Eagan. And tell Callum..." She fought back the rising swell of emotion in her throat. "Tell him good luck with everything—the alliance and his marriage and..."

Eagan saved her from embarrassing herself with more tears by giving her another curt nod. And then he was gone.

Dragging in a fortifying breath, Caroline slung the satchel across her body, then tied one end of the rope around her waist, as Eagan had suggested.

Fleetingly, she considered digging through the bag to make sure she truly did have enough supplies to make it to the Lowlands, but then she discarded the idea. Even if she was short an extra pair of slippers or a loaf of bread, what would she do, go back into the castle and root around for the things she needed?

No, there was nothing left for her in there. She would just have to make do with whatever Eagan had packed.

She hurried to the dark row of fruit trees at the back of the garden, sizing them up for the thickest branches and the closest reach to the top of the wall. None was particularly sturdy looking, but she selected one of the pear trees and quickly tied the other end of the rope around its trunk.

Carefully picking her footing, she began climbing. Luckily, she'd had plenty of practice over the years— being an outdoorsy tree-hugging type really did have its advantages here in the medieval era.

Though Eagan had told her to hurry, she cautiously tested each branch before putting weight on it. The last thing she needed was to fall and break her neck mere feet away from freedom.

She looked up at the wall through the moonlit leaves. It still seemed so far away. She had to keep going. Drawing a breath, she reached up for another branch.

Suddenly, a pair of hard hands closed around her waist.

"What the hell are ye doing?"

Chapter Nineteen

A scream caught in Caroline's throat, but it never escaped as she was pulled downward.

Callum plucked her from the tree as if she were just another ripe pear dangling from its branches.

"Let me go!" she gasped, struggling in his hold.

He lowered her to her feet, but his hands remained tight around her waist. With one step, he backed her into the deep shadows beneath the tree. Her shoulder blades bumped against the castle's stone wall. Callum loomed over her, a dark figure outlined in silver moonlight.

"What the bloody hell are ye thinking?" he snapped. He grasped the rope tied around her waist and yanked it away. "Are ye mad, climbing like that in the dead of night? Ye could have killed yerself."

"I would've been fine."

His eyes, which seemed to glow gold in the dimness,

locked on the satchel hanging across her body. "Ye were trying to leave," he said slowly.

She lifted her chin. "Yes."

"What the hell, Caroline?" he growled. "Ye promised ye wouldnae attempt to escape again."

"And *you* promised to take me to Leannan Falls when I proved to you that I'm from the future!"

"And I *will*. But I cannae just set Laird MacConnell aside and ride out with you. If I leave now, the alliance —everything I've worked for as Laird—may fall apart."

"How long before you'll let me go?" she demanded.

He breathed a string of curses. "I dinnae ken."

"So what do you expect me to do?" she shot back. "Just sit around twiddling my thumbs until you marry Aileas?"

"Nay." His voice was low and grating. "Caroline, I willnae—"

She couldn't take any more of this. "I can't stay here! Don't you get it? I can't watch you making plans to marry someone else. It's killing me inside. So let me go. To hell with the MacBeans and your responsibility to protect me. Let me go to the falls by myself. My sisters need me, and there's nothing here for me anymore. I just can't…I can't…"

Her breaths were coming fast and shallow. She sucked in air in great gulps, as if she'd been trapped underwater and had just broken the surface. Except instead of relief, she felt as though she was being squeezed from every side.

"Let me go," she panted again. "For both our sakes."

He planted his hands on either side of her, barricading her against the wall with his muscle-corded arms and broad chest. "Nay," he repeated. "I willnae. I *cannae*."

"Callum—"

"I am no' going to marry Aileas."

"What? But your alliance—"

He moved closer, and she could feel the heat and frustration radiating from his powerful body.

"I will find another way. I *have* to. Dinnae ye understand, Caroline? I cannae marry another when I love *ye*."

"You..." The whole world went quiet except for the rush of blood in Caroline's ears. Her heart stuttered, then hammered hard against her ribs. "You love me?"

"Aye. I love ye, Caroline. I am mad with loving ye, wanting ye, *needing* ye."

"I love you too," she breathed. "God, how I love you."

In less than a heartbeat, he'd closed the distance between them. He yanked the satchel over her head and tossed it aside, then pressed her into the stone wall, his hands in her hair, around her waist, gripping her hips. When his lips found hers, it was as if her whole body had been set aflame.

This time, there was nothing gentle about his kiss. It was demanding and fierce, stealing her breath and sending need spiraling through her. She surrendered to him, to the wild torrent of sensations. He invaded her mouth with his velvet tongue, delving deep and tangling with her in an erotic promise of what was to come.

And this time, she knew, there would be no drawing back, no pulling away.

His hands slid up her waist to her breasts, cupping and kneading her. But it wasn't enough, for he reached up and tugged at the neckline of her gown. She heard a lace on the back of her dress pop, but she didn't care, for in the next moment, the cool night air brushed over her exposed breasts.

Just as swiftly, he broke their kiss and dipped his head to drag his hot tongue over one pearled nipple.

Caroline sucked in a hard breath. "*Yes.*" She sank her fingers into his hair as he teased her with his tongue. A hand rose to cup her other breast, the calluses on his palms sending electric jolts of pleasure through her.

With his hips pinned against hers, she could feel the hard length of his cock already straining against his trews. But when she reached down for him, he moved out of her grasp.

"I've dreamt of tasting ye," he rasped, dropping to his knees before her. "And then of feeling ye come undone when I'm inside ye."

God, yes. She leaned against the wall, uncaring of the stones biting into her back as he dragged her skirts up.

She shivered as the air brushed her bare thighs above her stockings. When he had her skirts bunched around her waist, he touched her there, running his fingers along her sensitive skin. Her knees quaked until he gripped one of her hips, steadying her.

And then she felt the hot fan of his breath right against her sex, and she nearly came undone. He waited, drawing out the delicious anticipation until she wanted to rock forward against his poised lips. But then he flicked his tongue along her damp folds, and all thoughts of moving vanished. Only his hand on her hip kept her from crumpling into a boneless heap.

He parted her slowly, his tongue teasing that spot of pure pleasure in a torturous exploration. A moan rose in her throat. Her head fell back against the stones, lashing from side to side as he teased and caressed, tasted and delved with his tongue.

His other hand rose and skimmed over her thigh, then hooked under her knee, hoisting her leg over his shoulder. With her even more exposed to him, he deepened the strokes of his tongue, drawing a whimper from her. Her back arched off the wall, her hips beginning to undulate.

His hand slid up along her bent leg once more and joined his mouth on her sex. One finger circled her entrance slowly, tormenting her with the yearning for more until she found herself begging him.

"Please," she panted. "Now, Callum. *Please*."

He abruptly jerked to his feet with a groan, one hand flying to his trews. When he yanked them out of the way, his cock sprang free, thick and rigid with need.

He lifted her leg once more, hooking it over his hip, then took himself in hand, guiding the head of his cock to her entrance.

But then he froze, his manhood nudging but not entering her.

"Tell me ye want this," he breathed.

"Yes. I want this. I want *you*."

With a feral growl, he drove forward, taking her

fully. She gasped as he filled her, stretched her, claimed her.

Suddenly he lifted her fully off the ground, his hands splayed over her bottom to hold her up. She looped her other leg around his waist, latching her ankles behind his back and sinking her fingers into his taut shoulders.

He pinned her against the wall, holding himself deep within her for a long moment. And then he began to move, drawing out and plunging back inside her with slow, deliberate thrusts. Each one stole a little gasp from her, coiling her need tighter and tighter.

"I have wanted this—wanted ye—from the first moment I saw ye," he ground out. He began driving into her faster. "Wanted to make ye *mine*."

"I am," she moaned. "*I am yours*."

His control began to slip. He thrust harder now. With each pounding invasion of his cock, his chest rasped against her bare breasts, shooting pleasure through her. Her hands turned to claws on his shoulders as the sensations spiraled higher and higher.

Her breath hitched, and suddenly she shattered into a thousand shards of pure ecstasy. She cried out his name, clinging to him as the storm of pleasure broke over her.

A heartbeat later, he thrust hard and deep once, twice, and then he was tumbling over the edge with her, grinding into her and growling her name.

As they drifted back to earth, he pressed his forehead to hers, their hearts thudding and their slowing breaths mingling.

Gently, he lowered her to her feet, letting her skirts

fall back around her ankles. But instead of stepping away, he gathered her in a tender embrace, nuzzling her ear through her hair.

"Caroline," he murmured. "Dinnae run away from me. I…I ken ye still wish to go home to yer sisters."

The words made her chest compress painfully, squeezing the air from her lungs. "Yes," she whispered, fresh tears pricking her eyes.

"I will see ye safely returned to them—or at least to Leannan Falls. But please dinnae try to go just yet. Let me have whatever time I can steal from ye." He touched her cheek, her hair, brushed her lips with his thumb. "Let me call ye my own until I settle matters with MacConnell. Then I'll take ye to the falls myself."

"And…and what of the marriage alliance?"

"I meant what I said before—I willnae marry Aileas. Even after…" He swallowed, his throat bobbing. "Even after ye leave, I cannae marry another when I love ye. I will just have to find a different way forward with Laird MacConnell."

Stealing time. That was what they were doing. Even without the marriage alliance, they didn't have a future. But whether they had a day or a week or a month left together, she wanted to give it to him—wanted to give *all* of herself to him.

"Yes," she murmured again.

She gazed upon the solid line of his jaw, softened only slightly by the touch of moonlight, his warm, firm lips, the muscular column of his neck. His eyes burned into hers like glowing shards of amber.

She was dooming herself to a shattered heart.

But if it meant she could hold on to this beautiful, strong, honorable man for a little while longer, so be it.

Eagan watched from his chamber window as two figures shifted and emerged from the shadows at the back of the garden. The Laird and Caroline stepped into the moonlight and strode toward the garden's open gate.

Callum carried the rope and satchel Eagan had given Caroline in one hand. His other hand was entwined with the woman's.

Eagan hissed a curse. How could his plans have crumbled yet again?

What a disaster this day had been.

A sennight past, he'd composed an anonymous missive to Laird MacConnell. In it, he'd warned the Laird that he ought to mind his alliance with the MacMorans more closely instead of taking it for granted. And he'd added that MacConnell might not be pleased to learn that another woman had been occupying Laird MacMoran's attentions of late. If he still hoped to marry his daughter to Laird MacMoran, mayhap Laird MacConnell ought to remind him of their agreement.

He hadn't intended for the hotheaded Laird MacConnell to come barreling straight for Kinmuir, feathers puffed out with threats of breaking the alliance all together. What was worse, he hadn't realized until that morning that Callum was intending to return Caroline to her home that very day.

If Callum had left a few hours earlier, or if Laird MacConnell had arrived a few hours later, then Caroline would effectively no longer be Eagan's problem. But Callum had never made mention of escorting Caroline personally to the Lowlands, and MacConnell was quick to anger—and even quicker to arrive at Kinmuir.

And Eagan *still* hadn't gotten rid of the damned woman. When he'd seen her slip into the garden earlier that night, he'd seized the opportunity to right his failed plans. She'd been ready to leave, too, damn it! She'd only needed a few words of encouragement and the supplies he'd thrown together, and she would have been gone from his life for good.

But somehow only moments after Eagan had slipped back into the keep and quietly closed himself into his chamber to watch her scale the wall and disappear into the night, the Laird had shown up. And judging from the way they walked shoulder to shoulder, their fingers intertwined, they were more intimately entangled than ever.

Blast it all! At every turn, his plans had gone awry. It was almost as if fate was taunting him with his inability to be rid of the interfering woman.

But why did he deserve fate's wrath? He only sought what was best for his clan. Caroline was blinding the Laird, making him selfish and short-sighted. Someone had to remind him of his responsibility.

Eagan had tried. He'd sent the missive nudging MacConnell to take heed when it came to his alliances.

He'd urged the Laird to allow Caroline to depart on her own, or to send her with a contingent of men in order to permit Callum to remain with MacConnell. And he'd all but opened the castle gates for Caroline, giving her everything she'd need to leave.

But it hadn't been enough. He'd been thwarted by bad luck and poor timing every step of the way.

He swiped a hand over his face, stepping back from the window as Caroline and the Laird continued toward the keep's doors and out of his view. He had tried to be subtle, tried not to act too brashly for fear of overstepping his role as seneschal.

Mayhap that was the problem. He needed to be more decisive, take a bolder course of action.

He moved back to the window, staring blankly down at the darkened garden below. Aye, it was time to become more brazen. As a gentle breeze ruffled the plants under his gaze, he began to formulate a new plan.

Chapter Twenty

Callum clenched his hands against the desire to reach across the high table and pull Caroline into his lap.

They'd agreed that when they were in Laird MacConnell's presence, it was best to pretend that naught had changed, that Caroline was only Callum's guest and that he was still negotiating in good faith with MacConnell about their alliance.

But *everything* had changed last night. He loved Caroline. She loved him. And when they had been joined as one, he knew he could never let her go.

But of course he would have to, once matters with MacConnell were settled suitably enough for him to take her to the Lowlands. Frustrated bile burned up the back of his throat at the thought.

He took a bite of porridge and swallowed against it. He would deal with that when it came. For now, he had to convince the recalcitrant Laird MacConnell to let go of the notion of a marriage between Callum and Aileas to seal their alliance.

Except for the clatter and noise of the morning meal being served, the high table was silent. MacConnell sat next to Callum, his daughter on the other side of the table. And because he had wanted to maintain the appearance that Caroline was his guest, Callum had seated her next to Aileas.

"I trust ye slept well, Laird?" Callum broached.

MacConnell's only reply was a grunt. He kept his head lowered over his bowl of porridge, a scowl pinching his grizzled features.

Callum glanced at Caroline. Her lips were pressed together and her brows lifted with uncertainty. Hell, there was no point in dancing around it.

"Dinnae ye think it striking that Girolt MacBean was in all likelihood the one to send ye that missive, Laird?" Callum began pointedly. "It makes perfect sense, of course. Kenning that our clans' union is *strong* and *solid*, he seeks to undermine it by causing discord between us."

"The only thing causing discord at the moment, MacMoran, is *yer* resistance to the most obvious course of action—the one yer father and I agreed upon three years past."

Callum gritted his teeth. Bloody hell, would the man make him rehash their entire argument yesterday?

"Mayhap a marriage—or several marriages— between our clans would indeed help us both feel more…confident in our alliance," Callum tried again. "We might host a tournament together. Men and women of both clans could mingle that way. And many a match started at a tourney leads to—"

MacConnell pinned Callum with a fierce stare. "Is there something wrong with my daughter, MacMoran?"

Across the table, Aileas's eyes rounded. "Father, please, dinnae—"

"Is that what all this hemming and hawing is about?" MacConnell went on, ignoring his daughter's rapidly reddening face. "Do ye find some fault with my bonny, sweet Aileas? If so, speak, man, so that I may set ye straight with my fists!"

"Nay, Laird, this has naught to do with yer daughter," Callum said.

But even as he spoke, Aileas pushed back from the table. Her cheeks had suddenly gone starkly pale. She pressed her fingers over her lips and lowered her watery blue eyes, then hurried toward the hall's doors.

MacConnell harrumphed at her abrupt departure, shooting daggers at Callum with his eyes as if he'd been the one to embarrass her so.

Hesitantly, Caroline rose from the table. Her gaze shifted between Callum and MacConnell. She seemed to decide something, for she gave a little nod. "I'll go speak with her."

With a swish of blue skirts, she was gone, leaving Callum alone with the obstinate Laird.

CAROLINE FOUND Aileas in the garden. She was bent

over beneath one of the plum trees, spitting and wiping her mouth with the sleeve of her gown.

"Are…are you all right?"

Aileas straightened, kicking dirt over the ground where she'd just been sick. When she faced Caroline, her skin was pale and clammy, and her eyes brimmed with tears.

"Forgive me for leaving so abruptly, Mistress Caroline. I hope I didnae offend ye or Laird MacMoran by—"

Aileas cut off abruptly, pressing a hand over her mouth and swallowing hard.

"You can just call me Caroline," she said as the younger woman fought to regain her composure. "And are you really all right? I could send for the village healer. She might be able to—"

"Nay, that isnae necessary," Aileas replied. "I am merely worked up, is all. My nerves have been wound too tight ever since my father declared we were to ride immediately to Kinmuir to settle the matter of the marriage alliance. All this arguing and strain puts my stomach in knots. When my father is in a state like this, he willnae listen to anyone."

The girl's voice broke on the last word, and she choked back a sob. A few tears slid down her cheeks.

Caroline approached slowly. "He certainly isn't listening to Callum, that's for sure. Your father is no doubt chewing him up right now. I hope there's something left of him when we get back inside."

At Caroline's awkward attempt to lighten the mood, Aileas gave a weak laugh, but then her pretty features fell once more. "If his own daughter cannae get through to him, I dinnae see what chance Laird MacMoran stands."

Caroline stilled. This whole time, she'd been thinking of Aileas as...if not her enemy, then at least an adversary. Aileas was beautiful, sweet, and meant to be Callum's wife. Jealousy and pain had burned in Caroline's gut with that knowledge.

Yet now she realized how small and petty she'd been to direct such feelings toward the other woman. Aileas didn't seem to want this marriage alliance either, and was so distraught over her father's behavior that she'd made herself sick. But as a woman of her time, Aileas had no say in the matter, no voice. No choice.

Caroline laid a gentle hand on Aileas's arm. "Maybe it would help to talk about it?"

Aileas hesitated, but then she fixed vibrant, tear-filled eyes on Caroline and nodded.

Caroline led them to a wooden bench that sat against the garden wall beside the climbing rose. Warm morning sun drenched them as they settled next to each other.

"What do you wish your father would listen to you about?" Caroline began.

"It's this marriage alliance." Aileas shook her golden head, her brows knitted. "It is obvious that Laird MacMoran doesnae wish for it to go forward. But Father willnae drop it. To be pushed onto the Laird when he clearly doesnae want to marry me—it is humiliating. But that isnae even the worst of it."

"What is?"

Aileas lips trembled. "It is...kenning that there is someone who *does* want me more than aught in the world. And I want him, too. But...but we will never be..."

She dropped her face into her hands as quiet sobs shook her shoulders.

Caroline was stunned into silence for a long moment. Belatedly, she looped her arm around Aileas and squeezed her shoulder, as she would have done for one of her sisters if they were upset.

"You're...you're saying that you're in love? With someone you can't be with?"

Though Aileas was from a different century and country, *that* was something Caroline could relate to. Her heart ached in sympathy, an echo of Aileas's pain.

"Aye," the girl said shakily, lifting her head from her hands. She dashed the tears from her cheeks, but more flowed down. "My love longs to marry me, but my father would never allow it."

"Have you told your father about this man?"

"Nay!" Aileas squeaked. "He would likely kill him, and start a clan war in the process—my love is from a different clan, ye ken. And even if he were-nae, my father is too fixed on this marriage alliance."

Caroline frowned. From what little she knew of Laird MacConnell, she could understand Aileas's trouble in getting the stubborn, bull-headed man to listen.

"What if you found a way to delay the marriage alliance? It could give you and Callum time to figure out an alternative that would work for both your clans—and keep your father happy."

"I already have. A year past, my father thought to make the arrangement official with Laird MacMoran, but my mother and I managed to convince him that I was still too young. I'd hoped that in time, I would come up with a solution to this muddle, but I havenae—and now my father willnae be delayed any longer."

Caroline let a long breath go. For all of her frustration and grief over the predicaments facing her—her longing to return to her sisters, her growing love for Callum, the increasing rift she felt inside as she was pulled in two different directions—Aileas's struggles were worse. How harsh it seemed to force two people to marry when neither wanted it. And how cruel that Aileas got no say in her own future, her own life.

She'd been wrong in making Aileas out as some sort of rival, even only in her own head. But now she could make it right. She could stand up for Aileas, fight for her the way she'd fight for her sisters.

Caroline took Aileas's hands in hers and gave her a little squeeze.

"We're going to figure this out," she said. "I promise. You shouldn't be forced to marry Callum. There has to be another way to join your clans without a marriage. With you, me, and Callum all working on it, I'm sure we can find a solution."

Aileas blinked back some of her tears. "Truly?"

"Yes."

"But...why? Dinnae think me ungrateful," Aileas said hurriedly. "But why are ye helping me?"

Caroline smiled faintly. "You know your 'someone special'? The one who wants you more than anything in the world, and you want him right back?"

Aileas nodded.

"Well, I think…that's how Callum and I feel about each other."

Aileas's big blue eyes went round. "There *is* something between ye! I kenned it."

Heat crept into Caroline's face. Her gaze drifted to the spot against the back wall where only a few hours ago, Callum had told her he loved her, driven deep inside her, claimed her heart, body, and soul.

Giving herself a little shake, she tore her eyes away and focused on Aileas once again. "Callum already told me that he would find a way to put a stop to this arranged marriage. Knowing that you want the same thing only makes it clearer that you two can't marry. I'm really helping both of you. But…it's more than that."

"Oh?"

"This world can be tough," Caroline said, adding softly, "especially in this era." She shot Aileas a lopsided grin. "Us girls have to stick together."

Aileas gave her a wobbly smile in return. "Thank ye."

"Come on," Caroline said, standing from the bench. "We'd better get back to the great hall. Laird MacConnell is probably in the process of turning Callum into minced meat, and we need him in one piece if he's going to help us convince your father."

Chapter Twenty-One

E agan waited in the east tower stairs just outside the great hall. The rest of the castle's inhabitants had given the hall and the two quarrelling Lairds a wide berth. But Eagan had lingered within earshot, waiting for his opportunity.

The Laird and MacConnell had spoken in circles nigh all day. To Eagan's grave disappointment, Callum was arguing against a marriage alliance—the marriage alliance Duncan had concocted for the betterment of both clans. And in the name of peace, for with the MacMorans and the MacConnells united, the MacBeans would be forced back into their place.

Callum had truly forgotten his responsibility. And there was only one explanation for why the Laird would do such a thing. It was the woman. Caroline had clouded the Laird's mind, twisting him away from the right course of action.

Would the Laird ever take her to her homeland, wherever that was? Based on what Eagan had seen last night, it was becoming increasingly unlikely. Callum would destroy his alliance with MacConnell, all to keep the woman at his side.

Unless Eagan did something to drive her out.

And to do so, he needed the perfect moment to set his plan in motion. He'd almost slipped out of the hall earlier during the morning meal, but blessedly he'd hesitated. If he hadn't, MacConnell's daughter and Caroline would have come upon him, and his plan would have fallen apart.

But now that the hours had stretched and the evening meal was nearly upon them, time was almost out. Callum, Laird MacConnell, Aileas, and Caroline were all still rooted at the high table. And Tilly and the other kitchen lasses had turned to their preparations. He wouldn't get a better opportunity than this.

With a fortifying breath, he slid from the shadows in the stairwell and skirted the edge of the great hall toward the keep's doors, trying to avoid notice. To his relief, the four at the high table were still so involved in their discussion—which mostly involved MacConnell demanding that the marriage alliance go forward and Callum suggesting alternatives—that they paid him no heed.

Once he was out of the keep, Eagan breathed a little easier, but he still glanced around cautiously to make sure no one took note of his presence. Satisfied that he hadn't been observed, he strode toward the garden. He slipped through the gate, his gaze immediately landing on what he sought.

Hurriedly, he plucked what he needed, clenching one hand to conceal what he'd taken. Then he hastily crossed through the gate again.

He glanced at the side door leading to the back of the kitchens. It would be more direct that way, but then again, it would appear suspicious for him to use that door when he normally didn't. So instead he headed back to the keep's double doors and ducked inside.

Somehow he managed yet again to avoid notice as he crossed the hall and pushed through the swinging door to the kitchen. Inside, he found a riot of activity as Tilly and the others prepared the evening meal. It was to be a simple stew, perfect for Eagan's purposes.

"How soon until the meal is ready?" he asked Tilly. His hand began to sweat around what he clutched. He only hoped his voice sounded natural.

"Just as fast as I can make it," Tilly replied tartly, not even looking up from a carrot she was chopping.

"The Laird is asking for it to be served now," Eagan lied. "He doesnae want to keep his guests waiting."

Tilly squawked like an aggravated goose. "Gracious me! I suppose I can send the stew out, but the bread isnae ready yet."

"The bread can wait. I'd serve the stew now if I were ye."

With a mournful cluck of her tongue at being rushed, Tilly tossed the carrot she'd just chopped into a bubbling, fragrant caldron of stew that hung over the kitchen's enormous hearth. She snapped out orders to several lasses, calling for bowls and a tray. As one lass ladled the stew, another placed the full bowls on a tray, while still more scurried to keep out of the way.

Margaret took the tray and hastened toward the swinging door to the hall, but Eagan stepped in her path.

"I'll take these out. Yer mother needs ye more in here."

"Thank ye, Eagan," Tilly called over the noise in the kitchen. "That's verra considerate. And aye, Margaret, I need ye to keep an eye on…"

Eagan turned his back on them, and the bustle and din fell away. He could hear his heartbeat in his ears, hard and fast. Balancing the tray on one hand, he hunched over, shooting a quick glance over his shoulder to make sure no one was watching him. But all in the kitchen were too caught up in their own tasks.

Quickly, he opened his hand over one of the bowls and dropped in the leaves he'd plucked.

Foxglove leaves.

He snatched up one of the spoons placed on the tray and stirred in the leaves until they were suspended in the stew with the other vegetables and hunks of meat. Then he stuck a spoon in each of the other three bowls to make them appear the same.

Pushing through the swinging door, his feet carried him to the raised dais.

"…Might consider waiting until I am nineteen," Aileas was saying, her chin timidly tucked.

Bloody hell, even MacConnell's daughter was

speaking against the marriage alliance? Thank God Eagan was acting now, lest Caroline manage to warp Laird MacConnell's thinking on the matter as well.

Still, Aileas was just a lass, innocent in all this as far as Eagan could tell. Guilt cinched his gut tight. Yet he could not stray from his plan.

He set the bowl with the foxglove in front of Aileas.

Once he'd distributed the other bowls, he stepped down from the dais, but instead of hiding away again, he lingered in a corner, watching. He had to be sure his plan worked this time, and it might involve some…guidance on his part.

He could have simply poisoned Caroline, but that wouldn't have gotten rid of her—unless he'd sought to kill her. Eagan wouldn't go that far—not when he had his immortal soul to consider. Nay, he only wanted her gone, and making her ill would likely have the opposite effect, forcing her to remain while she recovered, all the while drawing the Laird's sympathy and attention.

But Eagan knew what lay between the Laird and Caroline. And he knew how women could be when they were jealous. Aileas was Caroline's rival for the Laird's hand. Wouldn't it make sense, then, for Caroline to try to get the lass out of her way? That was how it would look when they all realized Aileas had been poisoned with foxglove.

It was a shame to harm the innocent Aileas, but the matter at stake was bigger than one mere lass.

He watched, his breath catching in his throat, as the four on the raised dais halted their endlessly pivoting conversation and began eating in taut silence.

His gaze locked on Aileas. She lifted the spoon to her mouth.

But just as she was about to eat, the kitchen door swung open and Tilly came bustling out with a tray of steaming bread. As she stepped onto the dais, she cut off Eagan's view. Eagan cursed, straining to see around her wide hips, but it was no use.

"Apologies for the delay, Laird," Tilly said, setting the bread in the middle of the table.

When she stepped back, Aileas had lowered her hand and was scooping up another spoonful of stew.

She must have taken a bite, then. Eagan nearly sagged with relief. All was in motion now.

Aileas lifted the spoon to her mouth once more, but she hesitated. She swallowed hard, staring down at the stew, then set her spoon back down and rose shakily to her feet.

Good God, did foxglove truly work so quickly? Was she already feeling ill? Nervousness jolted through him. This was his moment to act.

He rushed to the high table, plastering a frown on his face.

"Are ye well, Mistress Aileas?" he asked, infusing his voice with concern.

"Aye," she replied, glancing at him. "Or…nay. I believe I need some air."

He let his gaze fall casually to her bowl of stew. Amazingly, a foxglove leaf was floating on top. This was too easy. After so many failed attempts to be rid of Caroline Sutton, it was as if fate was handing him the perfect circumstances.

"What is this?" he asked slowly. He used her spoon to fish out the leaf, then held it up dramatically.

He felt the eyes of the Laird, MacConnell, Caroline, and Aileas all lock on the leaf.

"Why…" He widened his eyes in an imitation of shock. "This is foxglove!"

Chapter Twenty-Two

Callum stood so quickly that his chair clattered backward onto the dais. Laird MacConnell did the same less than a heartbeat later.

"*Poison*," MacConnell hissed. "Someone put poison in my daughter's stew!"

"Father, I didnae—" Aileas began, but MacConnell cut her off.

"I'll have yer bloody head on a pike for this, MacMoran!" he roared, spinning toward Callum.

Callum had no doubt that he could best the older man physically, but if they came to blows now, any hope of an alliance would be quashed once and for all.

"Hold, man!" he snapped at MacConnell. He spoke loudly enough that MacConnell started, and Callum used the slim window of the man's hesitation to gain control of the situation.

He snatched the leaf from Eagan's fingers, staring at it closely. Caroline moved to his side to look as well.

"It *is* a foxglove leaf," she breathed, stunned.

"Who could have done this?" he muttered.

"Whoever it was, the villain is here under yer roof, MacMoran."

"Tilly prepared the meal, Laird," Eagan offered. "Mayhap we ought to question her."

"Tilly!" Callum bellowed, loud enough to rattle the great hall's rafters. His patience was already threadbare after a day spent arguing with Laird MacConnell. And now someone had put foxglove in his guest's food. There could be no room for confusion or doubt—he had to get to the bottom of this matter, or else all hope for peace was lost.

Tilly came scuttling into the hall from the kitchen, her eyes wide. "What is it, Laird?"

He held up the foxglove leaf as she approached. "*This* was in Aileas's stew."

As her gaze fixed on the leaf, she blanched. "Foxglove. Good heavens."

"How did it get there?" he demanded.

Tilly's mouth worked in dumbfounded silence for a long moment. "I-I cannae say, Laird."

"Cannae, or willnae?" MacConnell barked.

"Silence," Callum ground out. "As ye've mentioned, Laird MacConnell, this...*incident* took place under my roof, so it is my responsibility to root it out. Now, Tilly, how could this have gotten into Aileas's bowl?"

"I dinnae ken, Laird. I-I made the stew myself. I would never add such a plant to aught that I cooked in my kitchen."

"And the lasses who help ye?"

Tilly straightened to her full, if paltry, height. "Nay, Laird," she said firmly. "Those lasses dinnae have a devious bone in their bodies. They would never do such a thing."

"Ye said ye made the stew yerself," Eagan prodded. "Did ye also gather the ingredients?"

"Nay, I only used what was in the basket that..." Tilly's gaze locked on Caroline. "...That Mistress Caroline prepared for me from the garden."

They all turned to Caroline. Her eyes widened. "Tilly, you couldn't possibly think I put foxglove in your basket."

"Nay, mistress, of course n—"

"But ye do spend a great deal of time in the garden, do ye no', Mistress Caroline?" Eagan asked. "And isnae there foxglove growing there?"

"Let us go find out," MacConnell said, thumping down from the dais and tromping toward the keep's doors. Tilly, Eagan, and Aileas all hurried after him, but as Callum moved to follow, Caroline caught his arm.

"I didn't do this," she breathed. "I would never—"

"I ken it, lass," he said quickly. "And I'll fight to prove yer innocence. But we must get to the bottom of this."

She nodded dazedly, then they followed the others out of the keep. When they reached the garden, they all filed through the gate and down one of the dirt paths between the raised beds.

"There," Eagan said, pointing toward where several clumps of foxglove grew out of one of the beds. "And look—the leaves on that one have been torn."

It was true—several leaves were missing from one of the plants.

MacConnell rounded on Caroline, and on instinct, Callum stepped in front of her.

"Ye did this, didnae ye, lass?" he demanded, narrowing his eyes on her.

"That doesnae make sense," Callum shot back. "Why would Caroline harm Aileas?"

"Mayhap because she wants ye for herself." The Laird jabbed a finger at Callum. "Mayhap she thinks if she gets rid of my Aileas, ye will marry her instead. And mayhap she is right, for ye seem all too eager to toss aside the marriage alliance."

"Are ye accusing *me* of being behind this incident as well as Caroline?"

"Father, ye are wrong about—"

"I dinnae ken what yer play here is, MacMoran," MacConnell interrupted, glaring between Callum and Caroline. "But I am no fool. The lass has every reason to go after my daughter."

"Caroline isnae one of us," Eagan said quietly. "Ye mustnae forget that, Laird. Ye dinnae ken what she is capable of."

"No' this," Callum bit out. "And she may no' be a MacMoran, but I willnae let these accusations stand."

"They arenae mere accusations," MacConnell snapped, pointing to the foxglove. "There is *proof*."

Tilly wrung her hands in her apron. "Nay, I dinnae believe Mistress Caroline could do such a thing. I ken her, and she wouldnae—"

"Then how do ye explain that?" MacConnell demanded, jutting his finger at the foxglove once more.

"I didn't do it."

"But she had reason—"

"Enough, Laird MacConnell, or so help me—"

"*Might I speak?*"

Everyone fell silent at Aileas's shrill cry. Sometime during their arguing, she'd been crowded to the side, but they all parted to stare at her now. She stood with her hands clenched at her sides so tightly that they trembled.

"If any of ye care to know, I havenae been poisoned. I didnae even eat any of my stew."

Guilt at his inattention to Aileas's wellbeing swept Callum, followed by confusion. He hadn't been paying attention to whether or not she'd eaten the stew earlier —he'd been too focused on his own foul mood after a day spent quarreling with Laird MacConnell. But he did remember her standing from the table not long after the meal was served, looking wan and clammy.

"Ye...ye are well, then, daughter?" MacConnell asked awkwardly. From the color rising to his face, he felt even guiltier than Callum for completely ignoring his daughter's health while caterwauling about her being poisoned.

"Aye, thank ye for yer concern, Father," she replied tartly.

"But ye werenae feeling well," Callum said slowly. "Ye said ye needed some air." He went over the events again in his mind. Aye, Aileas had risen from the table, which had drawn Eagan over. And then Eagan had noticed the foxglove in her stew.

"That is true, but no' because of the stew, which I didnae eat," she repeated.

"What do ye mean, ye didnae eat the stew?" Eagan said, his gaze fixing intently on Aileas. "I saw ye take a bite."

"Nay, I felt queasy at the first whiff of it. I tried to have a spoonful, but I couldnae."

Tilly huffed a wee breath and patted down her wild nest of red hair. "There was naught wrong with the stew, I can assure ye that. Well, other than the foxglove in it."

"Aye, I'm sure it would have been excellent without the poison," Aileas said impatiently. "That is no' the reason I felt ill."

"Then what is?" MacConnell demanded, his bushy gray brows drawn together in confusion.

Aileas hesitated, casting a glance at Caroline. Callum still stood halfway in front of her, but she leaned out from behind him. Like MacConnell, her brows were knitted together, but they slowly eased and lifted as realization dawned across her features.

"Aileas…?" she murmured.

Aileas gave her a little reassuring nod, then turned back to her father. "I was ill because…because I am pregnant."

"*What?*" MacConnell breathed.

But Aileas continued before MacConnell could sputter more.

She squared her shoulders and lifted her chin. "Aye. With Terek MacBean's bairn."

Chapter Twenty-Three

Laird MacConnell stumbled backward, and he would have fallen if Callum hadn't darted forward and gripped the man by the front of his tunic.

For her part, Caroline's breath left her in a hard whoosh.

Of course. When Aileas had dashed from the great hall that morning and thrown up in the garden, it wasn't just nerves or distress over her father's brash behavior.

She was pregnant.

But Terek MacBean...

A memory of the man, dark-haired, keen-eyed, and of an age with Caroline, flashed through her mind. Caroline hadn't paid much attention to him, for Laird MacBean had dominated their brief meeting. But she did remember that Terek had tried to calm his father when he'd become heated with anger.

That was Aileas's special someone, the man she loved, and who loved her in return.

"*Nay*," Laird MacConnell rasped. "No daughter of mine will consort with a MacBean."

"I...I think they've already done more than consort, Laird MacConnell," Caroline said on a sputtering exhale.

MacConnell rounded on her, and though he had regained his feet, Callum kept his hands balled in his tunic.

"Easy," Callum warned.

Callum earned a glare from MacConnell for that. The Laird couldn't seem to decide at whom to direct his rage in that moment. He glowered between Callum, Caroline, and Aileas.

"My grandbairn will *no'* be a MacBean," MacConnell said to no one in particular.

Instinctively, Caroline moved to Aileas's side to face MacConnell.

"Ye can disown me, Father, but I love Terek. I cannae hide the truth any longer. Our bairn will be a MacBean *and* a MacConnell."

As if he were a balloon that had been popped, MacConnell suddenly deflated, sagging in Callum's hold.

"How...how can this be happening?"

"We met two years past," Aileas offered, gentling her tone. "When ye met with Laird MacBean about ending his raids along our border."

"The MacBeans are harassing MacConnell lands as well?" Caroline asked, glancing at Callum.

"Aye," he replied. "They use the same tactics as they do against the MacMorans—striking vulnerable border farms, stealing sheep and cows, and occasionally grain as well." He turned to MacConnell. "Though we have agreed on little these last two days, we *can* agree that an alliance would benefit both our clans in taking a stand against the MacBeans."

"But now that alliance cannae be forged by marriage," Aileas added, her voice soft but firm. "Terek has already asked for my hand many a time. I refused, fearing the consequences to our clans' union and yer wrath, Father, but now that there is a bairn, I cannae deny our love any longer. I will wed Terek."

"Nay!" MacConnell moaned.

"Ye would rather I bear a bastard, Father?"

At her words, MacConnell exhaled, making a sound close to a whimper. Caroline feared he might slump fully to the ground, but he managed to stay upright.

"Good God, daughter, what have ye done?"

"I have followed my heart—just as ye did, Father. Ye stole Mother from the Camerons for heaven's sake, and all because ye loved her. And dinnae imagine I am too innocent to notice the fact that I was born six months after ye married her."

MacConnell's face flushed a deep red, but Caroline couldn't tell if it was from anger or embarrassment at the verity of Aileas's words.

As he continued to sputter, Caroline turned to Aileas.

"Why did you tell everyone you're pregnant?" she murmured.

Aileas blinked. "Because it is the truth."

"Yes, but...you were keeping it a secret. To protect

Terek and your love—and your child." Caroline couldn't help but glance at Aileas's middle with a faint smile before returning her concerned gaze to the young woman's face. "Why reveal it now?"

Aileas took Caroline's hand and squeezed it. "My father and the seneschal were ready to declare ye a poisoner. If I didnae tell the truth, ye would have suffered. And we lasses have to stick together."

"Then no one tried to poison Mistress Aileas?" Tilly piped up, her red brows furrowed in confusion.

"Someone still put foxglove in her stew," Caroline said with a frown.

Just then, her gaze fell on Eagan, who had been slowly backing away from the group.

Callum must have noticed him, too, for he released Laird MacConnell's tunic at last and strode slowly toward Eagan.

"Explain something to me, Eagan," he said, his voice cold and flat. "Ye claim to have observed Aileas eating her stew, then when she grew ill, ye noticed the foxglove in her bowl. But Aileas never ate the stew. So how did ye find the foxglove so quickly? And why did yer mind go straight to the notion that Caroline had tried to poison Aileas?"

A dark thought struck Caroline then. Sure, Eagan had never seemed to like her, but would he really try to frame her for poisoning?

Eagan continued backing up as Callum slowly advanced, until the seneschal bumped into the garden's stone wall. His blue-gray eyes were wide as his gaze flicked desperately over them all.

"I...ye dinnae..."

"Well?" Callum snapped, halting before Eagan, close enough that he was effectively pinning the seneschal to the wall with his broad form. "Was it ye, Eagan? Did ye put the foxglove there?"

Abruptly, Eagan's face crumpled and he slumped against the stones. "I was trying to *help* ye, Laird," he breathed in a rush. "The woman was distracting ye from yer duty—risking yer alliance with Laird MacConnell and the peace yer father worked so hard for! Ye needed to be rid of her, but she'd clouded yer mind so much that ye couldnae even see it. I was only trying to give ye reason to send her away so that ye could focus on yer negotiations with Laird MacConnell!"

"By poisoning my sweet daughter?" MacConnell demanded, regaining some of his indignant outrage from earlier.

"I didnae mean for any real harm to come to her," Eagan replied, staring wide-eyed between Callum and MacConnell. "I used the leaves of the foxglove rather than the flowers. She would have gotten sick, aye, but it wouldnae have killed her."

Callum shot a glance at Tilly over his shoulder. "Is that true?"

"Aye," the cook said grudgingly. "A few leaves wouldnae kill the lass, only make her ill." Then she frowned. "I dinnae ken what it would do to a woman carrying a bairn, though."

Aileas sucked in a breath and brought shaking fingers to her lips. "Thank God I didnae actually eat any of the stew."

"I didnae ken about the bairn, I swear!" Eagan pleaded.

"But ye still tried to poison my daughter," MacConnell barked. It seemed that with someone else to direct his rage at, the Laird was rapidly forgetting his anger at Aileas and the MacBean offspring she carried.

"And ye thought to paint Caroline as the villain in yer scheme," Callum went on, narrowing his eyes at Eagan.

"Laird, she is an outsider, no' one of us," Eagan implored. "Yer duty—"

"Dinnae lecture me on *my* duty," Callum thundered. "I ken my role. I am yer Laird, Eagan. Yet ye thought *ye* kenned better than I what our people need."

"I-I beg yer forgiveness, Laird," Eagan said, cowering against the wall. "I only thought to help the clan."

Callum let a sharp breath go, clearly trying to calm himself. He turned and met Caroline's gaze, his eyes blazing with fury for Eagan. But they also bore a shadow of…guilt.

Caroline felt it, too. Though Eagan was horrifyingly wrong in his methods, his motives weren't evil. He'd sought to protect the clan and ensure peace.

And the truth was, she and Callum *had* threatened that peace. He'd been ready to dissolve a marriage alliance without a clear alternative to placate Laird MacConnell. And she'd selfishly pursued her desire, her love for Callum, without thought of the consequences to him and his people once she returned to her own time.

What was more, a part of her had enjoyed dallying

here, savoring the feeling of belonging, of being needed, *wanted*. She'd let herself indulge in the simple pleasures and joys of life at Kinmuir—life with Callum—when her sisters probably thought she was missing or dead.

Unbidden, shame tightened her throat and burned behind her eyes. She'd made a mess of things, just as she had when she'd dropped out of school, and just as she had when she'd abandoned her parents' flower shop. She'd always had someone else to clean things up, to make things right—her parents, her sisters, and now the man she'd come to love.

But it was time for her to clean up her own messes, to set aside her selfish longings and help Callum secure a future for himself and his people—without her.

And it was time to own up to her responsibility to keep her family together.

It was time to go home.

Chapter Twenty-Four

C allum rode hard through Kinmuir's gates, reining in his horse in a spray of dirt and pebbles. He leapt from the saddle, tossing the reins to a lad who scrambled upright from his relaxed slouch against the side of the stables, eyes wide at his Laird's abrupt arrival.

Aye, he was eager to lay eyes on Caroline after a day spent away from the castle. Callum resented every moment apart from her, and every interruption that separated them. But he had to admit, in this case the task that had kept him was a worthy one. Anxious excitement coiled through him at the prospect of telling her about it.

As expected, he found her in the garden. She was just straightening from a crouch beneath the climbing rose, where she'd been tying it to the wooden trellis behind it with bits of twine. Not noticing him in the gateway, she arched her back and dragged the sleeve of her moss green gown over her forehead, admiring the rose for a moment.

He crossed his arms over his chest and leaned against the stone wall, letting himself drink in the sight of her. She was a soothing balm and a blazing fire all at once, somehow managing to make him feel calm and aflame at the same time. Her hair shone like a polished chestnut in the summer sun, her cheeks faintly flushed from her exertions.

But he wanted to feel the heat of her pale blue eyes on him, so he cleared his throat.

She whirled, her face lighting up like a dawning sky when her gaze landed on him. She wiped her hands on the apron tied over her gown and began to hurry toward him, but he stepped fully into the garden, moving to her so that they could remain in her favorite place.

"You're back," she said, searching him with her gaze. "How did it go?"

Two days past, when Aileas had revealed that she carried Terek MacBean's bairn and Eagan's plot to be rid of Caroline had been exposed, Callum had sent a missive to Girolt MacBean requesting another meeting. Yesterday, the MacBean Laird's terse agreement had arrived.

And today Callum had accompanied Laird MacConnell, Aileas, and their contingent of MacConnell warriors to Loch Darraig for a *tête-à-tête* with the MacBeans.

"Surprisingly well," Callum replied. He guided her to the wooden bench beside the climbing rose. "Blood wasnae spilt, which is always the sign of a good start to a marriage."

They sat next to each other, close enough that his thigh brushed hers. The scents of rich soil, plant life, and sweet roses clung to her, drifting to him softly.

"Then Laird MacBean agreed that Aileas and Terek could marry?" she asked, her brows arching hopefully.

Callum smiled at her impatience. Then again, a hell of a lot had happened in the last two days, and much had been riding on this meeting.

After Laird MacConnell's initial shock at learning his daughter had been impregnated by his enemy's son, the man had turned surprisingly pliant under Aileas's gentle, sweet resolve to wed Terek. It seemed as though the concept that his grandbairn would be a MacBean was softened by the knowledge that his only daughter was going to become a mother soon.

But of course the bull-headed Laird's bluster had returned when he realized that Girolt MacBean might be even less pleased with the fact that his son had gotten a bairn on a MacConnell.

It had been Caroline's brilliant idea to point out that several of their problems could be solved if they could convince Laird MacBean to allow Aileas and Terek to wed.

The MacMorans and the MacConnells already enjoyed a peaceful, neighborly relationship—one that had been tested by recent events, aye, but which was still strong despite the lack of a marriage alliance.

And if the MacConnells and MacBeans were joined together through wedlock, the MacBeans would be brought in line both when it came to the MacConnells, and also their close allies the MacMorans. No warfare necessary, or forced marriages, just the union of two young people who already loved one another.

MacConnell had readily agreed, yet he'd been stubbornly certain that MacBean wouldn't be so easily convinced. But at least MacBean had been willing to speak with MacConnell.

"Dinnae ye want to hear the whole tale of what happened from start to finish?" Callum teased.

Caroline rolled her eyes. "A simple 'aye' or 'nay' would put me out of my misery—and then you can tell me all the details, of course."

"Verra well, then. Aye, he agreed to the marriage."

She exhaled, a bright grin curving her mouth. "Oh good. All right, now start from the beginning."

Callum chuckled. "Things were tense at first, as was to be expected. I'm glad I was serving as the arbiter, for things might truly have come to blows a time or two. But once both MacConnell and MacBean's blood cooled a wee bit, they allowed Terek and Aileas to speak."

"And they actually listened?"

"Aye, for both Aileas and Terek were verra clever in their approach. They spoke of peace between our three clans, and all that could be gained from an alliance. And then they mused on the bairn for a time, including what they might name the wee lad or lass. That turned MacBean in particular to porridge."

Caroline laughed, leaning her head back against the stone wall behind them. "I can't imagine that man—

either of them, actually—as a cooing, besotted grandfather. But I'm glad it worked."

"The negotiations will continue between MacBean and MacConnell regarding the marriage," Callum continued. "But both MacConnell and I wished to extract a pledge from MacBean to cease his raids and reiving along our borders from this day forth. When MacBean hesitated, I feared all our progress would be lost, but then Terek explained *why* the MacBeans had been stealing."

"Oh?"

"It seems a blight moved through their crops a few years back, and they still havenae recovered from that terrible season. To make matters worse, they are being pestered by the MacLeans on their northwestern border, who are stealing livestock from the MacBeans' already pinched herds. The MacBeans were going hungry. They stole grain and animals from us to put food in the bellies of their starving bairns."

Caroline's eyes widened with surprise and sadness. "That is awful."

"Aye, but at least now we ken the truth. Instead of sending Aileas to Terek with a dowry of coin, MacConnell will send grain instead, as he's had two strong harvest years in a row. And I pledged several of this spring's lambs and calves to them as well. A wedding gift of sorts—in exchange for MacBean's pledge that they will no longer raid along our border."

"Then you have the peace you've been working so hard for," Caroline said. "It has all worked out. Except…"

Her gaze drifted to the keep, and his followed.

"Have you decided what to do about Eagan?" she asked hesitantly.

He stared at the west tower, where Eagan had been locked in his chamber until Callum could determine an apt punishment for his former seneschal.

"Nay," he replied. "I dinnae believe he deserves death, despite his willingness to harm Aileas—and ye."

"That night you found me trying to escape over the wall. The night we…" She trailed off, her cheeks pinkening and her gaze drifting to the shade beneath the fruit trees at the back of the garden. She cleared her throat, tearing her eyes away. "For what it's worth, he could have hurt me if he'd truly wanted to, but he didn't. All he wanted was for me to leave."

"Aye, but I cannae trust him now—no' as seneschal, and no' even under my roof as a servant. No' when he thinks to usurp my position as Laird by assuming he kens better than I what is best for my people." He fixed her with a penetrating stare. "And no' when he seeks to take what is most dear to me."

Her gaze dropped to her lap for a moment, and the lingering flush on her cheeks told him she was moved by his fierce protectiveness. "I can see why you wouldn't want him in the clan anymore," she said at last. "But what will you do with him, then?"

Callum let a long breath go. "There is to be a tourney between several neighboring clans in a few sennights. I'll seek the counsel of the other Lairds there. At the moment, I am too angry to give Eagan a fair judgment, but he can remain in his chamber for a time until I determine what his punishment shall be."

Silence fell for a moment, but then Caroline shot him a half-smile.

"A real medieval tournament," she mused. "That would be a hell of a thing to see."

Slowly, he lifted one of her hands in both of his. He cradled it as if it were the most precious, delicate thing in the world.

"Ye ken, ye *could* see it if ye wished."

When their gazes met, her eyes shimmered with pain. "I know."

God, seeing her hurting was like a knife in his chest. "Is yer time truly so much better than this one, then?" he prodded teasingly, trying to draw a smile from her. "Ye must miss yer airplanes and yer…what was the bean drink called again?"

She breathed a chuckle. "Coffee," she supplied. "And yes, I miss a few things. You would understand if you'd ever experienced a hot shower with the turn of a knob." She sobered, meeting his gaze. "But I don't really care about losing indoor plumbing, or anything else from my time. I would stay here, if by some magic my sisters…"

Caroline dropped her chin, blinking back the tears welling up once more.

"And…and would it make a difference if I asked ye to stay?" he murmured. "If I asked ye to be my wife?"

Her breath hitched and her head snapped up. For the briefest moment, he basked in the clear, shining light of love in her gaze. But then she squeezed her eyes shut, her brow creasing in sadness.

"You know I can't stay," she whispered. "Even though I love you."

He lifted one hand to her face and dragged his thumb over the tear that had slipped down her cheek. "I ken it. Yer sisters are waiting for ye."

"I can't give up on them. I have to at least try to find a way back to them."

"Ye wouldnae be the woman I love if ye didnae care so deeply for yer family. But I want ye to ken…" He swallowed, but his voice still came out a low rasp. "I want ye to ken that I'll love ye for the rest of my days, Caroline Sutton. That ye'll live in my heart every moment until time or fate or God brings us together once more."

A sob broke from her throat then, and she surged into his arms. "I love you, Callum."

"I love ye, too, Caroline." He held on tight, as if he could keep her nestled against his chest for all eternity with the strength of his arms alone.

But nay, deep in his soul, he knew—he couldn't hold her here, selfishly basking in her love, if it meant she had to give up her family. Because what he wanted even more than his own happiness was *hers*. And her happiness would never be complete without her sisters.

Which meant it was time that they ride to Leannan Falls.

Chapter Twenty-Five

The landscape as they approached the falls looked different to Caroline. It was wilder and less orderly than it had been in the twenty-first century. And it seemed far more remote—hardly the quick jaunt from the bustling metropolitan city of Edinburgh that it had been when she'd driven there with her sisters.

Five days ago, she'd said her goodbyes to Tilly, Margaret, and the rest of the castle—including the garden—once again. Somehow it was even more painful than it had been the first time.

Their ride from Kinmuir Castle had been uneventful. Even though they'd made good time, the journey felt painfully slow. Every day, every hour, every minute, Caroline tortured herself over the decision she was making.

She meant what she'd said to Callum. She would give up everything from her time to stay here with him —*as his wife*, she thought, yet another wave of pain hitting her—except for the possibility that she could be reunited with her sisters.

It felt as though half of her heart was missing without them. Yet she knew that when she went back through the falls, the other half of her heart would remain here. With Callum.

She could only pray that someday, with time, the sensation of being torn asunder by love would ease. Yet the closer they'd drawn to the falls, the worse it had become.

She'd ridden the tame mare Callum had picked out for her most of the way. With so many hours spent in the saddle, she'd grown more comfortable on horseback. But this morning, she'd foregone mounting her own mare and instead had strode to Callum's horse's side.

On this last day of their journey, she'd ridden in his lap, her head resting against his shoulder. She didn't care what the half-dozen MacMoran warriors who'd traveled with them thought. Yes, she was stealing time, wringing all the tenderness and love she could from every last moment they had together.

She was beyond caring that it might make saying goodbye that much harder. All she knew was that each step of the horses' hooves brought her closer to the falls, closer to her own world. And farther away from Callum.

Whatever time they had left, she wanted to listen to his heart beat against her ear, breathe in the scents of soap and leather and fresh air that clung to him, feel the warm strength of his arms around her.

All too soon, though, the distant hum of the falls became a roar. They broke through the trees and the falls came into view only a dozen yards ahead. Just as she'd remembered, it surged in a frothy white mist of water into the clear blue pool below. The rocky rim around the pool was edged with spray-dampened moss that glistened in the bright sun.

As their little party reined in just on the other side of the tree line, Callum turned to his men.

"Leave us," he said to Bron. "I'll meet ye in the village we passed no' long ago."

Bron nodded solemnly, then turned to Caroline. "Safe journey, mistress."

Callum had avoided telling Bron and the others exactly how Caroline was going to get the rest of the way home from the falls—or where her home truly was. Yet his men hadn't missed the somber air hanging over their Laird, and they didn't press for answers.

"Thank you, Bron," Caroline replied through a tight throat.

The others reined their horses around, Caroline's mare in tow, and headed back the way they'd come, leaving Caroline and Callum alone.

The roar of the falls faded beneath the sound of Caroline's heartbeat pounding in her ears. This was it. It was time to say goodbye once and for all.

He dismounted, but when he lifted her from the saddle and set her on the ground, his hands lingered on her waist. He gazed down at her with warm honey eyes.

"Grant me a few more moments," he murmured. "Let me show ye my love for ye one more time."

The pain in her chest made it too difficult to speak, so she only nodded.

He pulled a length of his blue and red plaid from one of his saddlebags. Taking her hand in his, he moved closer to the falls, where the mist from the rushing water just kissed the mossy bank.

He spread the plaid over the moss, then drew her down beside him.

"I will remember this," he murmured, his amber eyes tracing every line of her face. "And this." He reached out, his fingertips skimming over her cheekbone, her jaw, brushing softly over her lips before delving into her loose hair. "And this."

He leaned forward, his mouth pressing against hers in a tender kiss. Tears burning in her eyes, Caroline looped her arms around his strong neck and drew him closer. She opened under his lips, letting their tongues slowly tangle in a velvet caress.

Despite the ache throbbing like a pulse in her chest, her blood heated at his kiss. His hands slid over her back, his palms firm and warm even through her wool dress and chemise. His fingers found the laces running down the back of her gown and began untying them.

As he worked, she traced the corded strength in his arms, his shoulders, his upper back. She threaded her fingers into his dark hair, dragging her nails against his scalp.

He groaned in response, his kiss growing deeper, more possessive.

With a final tug on her laces, she felt her gown loosen. He peeled it from her shoulders, revealing her linen chemise underneath. She shimmied and scooted up to her knees, helping him push the gown lower, until he yanked it free of her feet and she could settle by his side once more.

But now it was her turn, for he was still wearing far too many clothes. She grabbed two fistfuls of his tunic and pulled it over his head. The garment slid free easily, revealing his bare chest. He looked like a Greek statue or a demigod, all sun-gilded lines of hard muscle.

She didn't have long to gaze upon him, for he closed the distance between them once more, his hands skimming over her hips and waist, his lips finding her neck.

"I want to see ye," he rasped. "I want to brand yer beauty onto my mind so that I cannae ever forget."

He lifted her chemise up and over her head, leaving her naked before him. He sucked in a breath as his liquid gold gaze caressed her bare skin.

It was a warm day, yet a shiver of anticipation stole over her. Even if the sun hadn't been bright and intense overhead, Callum's gaze was hot enough to nearly set her on fire.

At her back, the soft spray drifting from the waterfall cooled her enough that she could keep her wits about her. She wanted to remember this, too. Remember everything about him.

She reached for his trews and undid the fastening. They both quickly kicked off their boots, then he pushed his trews off and tossed them aside.

When he stood before her in all his strong, masculine glory, she simply let herself stare for a long moment. His cock already jutted from him, rigid and long with desire. His thighs were powerfully muscled and sprinkled with dark, crisp hair beneath his lean hips. Under her gaze, his breaths came short and shallow, his eyes glazed with hunger.

She reached for him, and his restraint snapped. He moved so quickly to her that she gasped in surprise just before he claimed her lips with his. He kissed her deeply, yet he moved slowly, as if savoring every second.

Their first time together had been untamed, fierce. As he continued to delve and stroke with his tongue, Caroline burned with a need just as intense as before, but this time they both sought to make the moment last, to imprint every sensation and touch onto their souls forever.

When at last he dragged his lips to her throat, and lower to her breasts, Caroline moaned, letting her head fall back. He eased her down onto the plaid, laving her breasts and flicking her taut nipples with his tongue in a slow, torturously pleasurable exploration.

Once she was panting and writhing beneath him, he moved lower still, trailing kisses over her ribs and across her stomach, then down each leg. When he moved back up and settled his shoulders between her knees, her legs were trembling.

Gently, reverently, he parted the damp folds of her sex and kissed her there. She arched off the plaid with a sharp exhale, fighting to make the pleasure last. But soon the sensation began to mount, pushing her toward the edge of release. She grasped his arms and drew him up the length of her body, cradling his hips between her thighs.

"Now," she breathed. She closed her hand around

his cock, feeling the surge of his desire there, the smooth hardness that would soon be filling her.

He let her guide him to her entrance, but when she released him, he took control. He gripped her hips, holding himself poised yet motionless against her. His amber wolf's eyes scorched her, claimed her, branded her as he gradually drove inside, taking her inch by aching inch.

When he was buried to the hilt, he rocked his hips in a slow circle, turning each of her panting breaths into a moan. He leaned over her, capturing her cries with his mouth, his tongue claiming hers in an erotic imitation of their lower joining.

Caroline fought to hold on to the moment, to make it last forever. But when Callum began thrusting in earnest, setting a slow rhythm that had her gasping and arching into him for more, she couldn't keep the tidal wave of pleasure at bay.

Her fingers sank into his taut buttocks as her whole body began to shake. She cried out his name as the surge of ecstasy broke over her, sending light and heat sizzling over every nerve ending.

He groaned his love for her over and over in her ear as he followed her over the edge. They tumbled as one, bound together in sensation for what felt like an eternity.

But all too soon, they drifted back to earth.

Callum lowered himself beside her and pulled her against his chest. He was warm and solid and so real. At her back, the falls' cool mist pricked her skin. The sun caressed their bare bodies. His heart thumped steadily against her cheek.

"I'll never forget," she whispered.

It was time. Tears rising to her eyes once again, she sat up and reached for her chemise.

"Do ye want to wear the clothes ye arrived in?" Callum asked quietly.

They'd brought her shorts and tank top in his saddlebags, but the idea of putting on those clothes seemed strange and dissonant to Caroline now. She'd gotten used to the comfort and functionality of her medieval garments.

"No," she replied, slipping the chemise over her head. "I'll just go in this." At least when she returned to the modern era, she'd have something to remember this time and place by. A scrap of linen to hold all her memories of this awe-striking experience.

Callum rose and dressed, a heavy silence hanging between them. Her gaze fixed on the falls, the rush of water filling her ears as she fought back the tears.

"Do ye want me to go to the top with ye?" Callum asked behind her.

Caroline swallowed. "No. I…I won't be able to jump if you are beside me."

"I'll stand here then, so I can watch ye all the way."

She nodded, then spun and threw her arms around him.

"I love you."

His warm hands held her close. "Promise me something."

"Anything."

"Promise me ye'll be happy in yer time. Spend time

with yer sisters. Forgive yerself for the guilt ye carry. And…" His voice pinched. "And find love."

She started to shake her head, barely holding back a sob, but he sank his fingers into her hair to still her. "Promise me. It is the only way I can let ye go—if I ken ye'll be happy."

"I promise," she choked out at last.

If she stood there another moment longer, she would never be able to leave, so she pulled away from his embrace and began striding up the forested slope toward the top of the falls.

Pine needles and twigs dug into her bare feet as she climbed, but she hardly noticed them. Tears blurred her vision. It felt as though her heart was being torn in two.

She'd been so sure that this was the right course of action, so convinced that it was her duty to keep her family together. She'd failed her sisters once by not keeping her parents' flower shop open—not putting the family first. She couldn't do so again.

But now as she reached the top of the falls, she wasn't sure of anything. What if she was throwing away the best thing that had ever happened to her—getting to live in this time and place, with Callum as her husband —for her own guilt?

She stepped to the edge where the water cascaded into the pool below. On the mossy bank, Callum stood, gilded in sunlight, staring up at her.

It had taken the loss of their parents to show Caroline just how valuable, and fleeting, life could be. And love. If she stayed, she would lose the only family she had left. But if she went, she would lose Callum forever.

An image of Hannah and Allie standing beside her above the falls flashed through her mind. She imagined their hands clasped in hers, just as they had been when they'd jumped the first time. It felt like a lifetime ago that she'd seen them, hugged them, laughed with them.

Callum knew her heart even better than she did. He'd known that her happiness couldn't be complete without her family. *Yer sisters are waiting for ye.* She had to know if they were all right. She had to try.

Caroline drew in a deep breath. "On the count of three," she murmured to herself. "One…"

I love you, Callum.

"Two…"

I love ye, Caroline.

"Three."

She squeezed her eyes closed, the image of Callum standing below, gazing up at her, burned into her mind.

And jumped.

Chapter Twenty-Six

Caroline's momentum pulled her deep into the pool. The whole world went quiet as water rushed into her ears.

But she didn't tilt or spin. There was no flash of light or sensation of being dragged down through a substance thicker than water. Only her descent into the pool, and then her drift upward.

She kicked toward the light streaming along the surface overhead. When she broke through, she took a deep gulp of air and blinked open her eyes.

"Caroline!"

Callum rushed toward the pool's edge, his amber eyes rounded in shock.

She was still here.

Elation and grief and confusion all hit her at once. Air whooshed from her lungs as if she'd been punched in the stomach. Her arms and legs stopped working, and she began to sink.

Just before her head dipped underwater, Callum's strong hands closed around her. He dragged her onto the pool's bank and into his arms.

"Caroline, ye're here. Ye're safe, lass. I've got ye."

Belatedly, Caroline realized she was weeping. Joy and sadness, triumph and loss tangling together in a maelstrom within her.

Some part of her had always known that jumping off the falls might not take her back to her own time. But she hadn't wanted to consider the possibility, for she wasn't sure if she should be resigned, hopeful, bereft, or simply relieved not to have the choice.

But now that the choice had been taken from her, she let herself truly grieve what it meant. This had been her only option, her only idea for how to return to her time—and her sisters. Its failure meant she would never see them again.

She wept for the loss of her sisters, for the blessing that was Callum, for all that she'd lost and gained in these few short weeks. For the woman she'd been before, and the woman she was now.

So much had changed. She wasn't the same as she'd been when she had dragged Hannah and Allie to the top of the falls, so eager for adventure. A part of her was missing now. But she'd grown in ways she could have never imagined before, her heart expanding to make room for not only the love of her family, but also of Callum.

She was still her parents' daughter, even after they were gone. And she would still be Hannah and Allie's sister, even if they never saw one another again.

Now, she was more than a daughter and a sister. She was also a woman in love, and the woman Callum MacMoran loved in return. She could be a wife. And maybe even a mother herself, someday.

As her tears began to ebb at last, she silently said her second goodbye of the day. She released the idea of ever returning to her time. Then she closed her eyes and pictured her sisters, one at a time, and said her farewells.

Wordlessly, she told them that she was all right, and that she would miss them every day. That they would always be together in her memories. And that she was sending them her love, across time and distance, forever.

When she opened her eyes, she found herself in Callum's arms. He'd wrapped her in his plaid and had pulled her onto his lap. He gazed down at her, his dark brows lowered in concern and emotion clouding his amber eyes.

"Speak to me, Caroline," he urged gently. "Are ye well? Tell me what I can do to ease yer pain."

"I'm all right," she mumbled through the last remnants of her tears. "Or at least I think I will be, in time."

"What…happened?"

She let a shaky breath go. "Nothing."

"I mean, what happened in *here*." He placed a hand over her heart. "And here." He touched her head. "Where did ye go just now?"

"I…I needed to let go," she replied. "Of the idea of returning to my time, and of…of being with my sisters again. I needed to say goodbye."

Callum pulled her into a hard embrace. "Ye are the

bravest, most noble-hearted woman I've ever kenned," he rasped into her hair.

As she hugged him back, the sharpest edge of her pain was softened by the love she felt for him. A sense of peace washed over her. She'd felt so unsure about what to do for so long, so lost. But whatever unseen force had brought her here had clearly decided that she was meant to stay. Her future was with Callum.

After a long while, he withdrew, fixing her with a searching gaze. "Ye will remain in this time, then?"

"Yes," she breathed. The anticipation, the excitement, the curiosity she'd tried to snuff out at the prospect of remaining here stirred to life like a fanned ember in her chest. The ache of loss was still present, but so too was a flicker of hope. "Yes, I'm staying."

"And...and do ye think ye can be happy here? With me?"

The uncertainty and hesitation in Callum's voice made Caroline sit up straight. She locked her gaze with his, ensuring that there could be no doubt about the truth of her words.

"Yes." Her throat tightened with another wave of emotion, but this time joy edged out the sadness as she spoke. "Callum, I love you. I want to build a life here with you."

He pulled in a breath. "Truly?"

"Yes, truly. I...I don't know what brought us together—fate, magic, God, or something else entirely. But whatever it was, I think I was sent here for a reason."

She shook her head in wonder, and she continued.

FALLING FOR THE HIGHLANDER

"Why did I jump through this waterfall in the twenty-first century, only to wake up in 1394—right where you would find me? And why can't I go back through time the same way I did before? Maybe because I'm meant to stay here—with you."

A slow smile spread over his face, and it was like the breaking of dawn, warm and promising.

"Aye, mayhap. I dinnae understand it either, but I *feel* it. We are bound together, Caroline. Our fates, our futures, are intertwined." He gave a soft chuckle. "And I am no' one to say such things lightly. I dinnae usually put much stock in magic or fate. A man must make his own destiny. But I cannae deny what I ken in my heart."

A soft laugh rose in her throat. And when he pulled her into another fierce embrace, she let the laugh grow and expand, until they were both shaking with it.

After a long while locked together on the waterfall's bank, Callum eventually released her and helped her to her feet. He kept her tightly wrapped in his plaid despite the warm day, for her chemise was still wet.

"Shall we go home, my bonny love?" he asked, taking her hand in his.

"Aye," she replied, doing her best impression of his rolling brogue.

Grinning, he turned to where he'd left his horse, but he halted abruptly.

"What is it?" she asked, trying to peer around his shoulder.

"There." He pointed past his idly grazing horse to the forest behind it. "That tent wasnae there when we arrived, was it?"

Sure enough, a small tent made out of colorful patches of cloth sat in between the trees not far off. An array of glazed pots, scraps of fabric, and other assorted items lay spread in display on the ground in front of it.

Caroline frowned. "I definitely didn't notice that before, but then again, we were rather…caught up."

Callum cast her a sideways glance before returning his attention to the tent once more. "There arenae many people out here. I cannae imagine that is a very good place to sell wares. Come. Mayhap the tent's owner is lost."

As they approached, Caroline noticed a small wagon behind the tent and a mule grazing nearby. A faint humming came from inside. When they were only a few paces away, a head abruptly popped through the tent's flap.

The head belonged to a woman with a cloud of frizzy gray hair and a wide, toothy grin. When the woman fixed her gaze on Caroline, she noticed that her eyes were two different colors—one green, one blue.

"I've been waiting for ye," she said, straightening and letting the tent flap fall closed behind her. Before it did, Caroline caught a glimpse of several bowls, dried herbs, and arranged rocks and crystals inside.

Callum was staring at her quizzically. "I am Laird Callum MacMoran, and this is Caro—"

"Och, I ken who ye are," the woman said with a wave of her hand. Her two-colored gaze pinned Caroline. "Ye are one of the three."

Caroline's heart did an odd little stutter. "Three what?"

"Three hearts. Three halves, made whole. Three women of the waterfall." She pointed a crooked finger toward the falls behind them.

The words hit Caroline like a blast of cold air, and her thoughts scattered like leaves. Her mouth fell open and she felt her eyes round.

Luckily, Callum had enough wherewithal to begin asking the woman questions.

"What do ye ken about the falls? And what do ye mean by three hearts?"

The woman planted her hands on her ample hips, a soft, knowing grin playing around her mouth. "Dinnae ye listen to the wise women when they tell their stories, Laird? Ye should, for the magic in Sweetheart Falls brought ye yer heart, yer soul." She glanced pointedly at Caroline.

Tilly's words rushed back to her. *Leannan means sweetheart, ye ken.*

"It...it was magic then," Caroline breathed.

The old woman cocked her head. "It was the faerie cursed to be trapped forever in the falls, but aye, close enough."

Caroline's head spun. Tilly had mentioned something about a doomed love between a faerie and a man, too. "A cursed faerie? And...and you're saying I was brought here because I'm Callum's...soulmate?" She glanced at him and found her wonder mirrored in his gaze. She *was* meant to be here.

The woman tipped her head toward the falls. "She was denied her love, ye ken, so she unites souls across time."

Caroline gave herself a little shake. The strange old woman was simply saying too many cryptic things to make sense of all at once. She opened her mouth, but the woman cut her off.

"I dinnae have all the answers ye seek, lass, for ye can find them yerself."

"What do you mean?"

"Ye seek the others."

"The others?" Caroline's heart leapt into her throat. "*My sisters?*"

"The three. The women of the waterfall," Callum murmured.

Caroline swallowed hard. "They fell through with me. Oh my God, could they be here, too?"

"Men came to me," the woman said, her gaze piercing Caroline. "Men from beyond the border—asking questions. About *ye.*"

"What men?" Caroline asked, her voice hitching.

"Saxford men."

"Saxford Castle isnae far from here—a few days' ride across the border," Callum interjected.

"What did they ask about me?"

The old woman smiled. "They asked if there were others like the one *they'd* found."

Her heart hammered wildly. "At least one of my sisters could be here. At Saxford." She spun to face Callum. "We have to go there. We have to see if it's true."

"Aye," he replied without hesitation.

Without thinking, Caroline bolted through the trees to where her wool gown and boots still lay on the banks of the pool below the falls. She tossed aside Callum's plaid and dragged the gown over her head, shoving her feet into her boots.

Callum appeared by her side, scooping up the plaid.

"We have to go—*now*," she breathed, her pulse racing and her head swirling with possibilities. Her sisters might be here after all. And then her heart, her happiness, could be complete.

"Aye," Callum repeated. "But hold a moment, love. Yer sisters will never forgive me if I let ye strangle yerself in yer own gown."

She'd gotten tangled in the laces on her dress, and it took him several precious minutes to free her.

"The woman said that the Saxford men had only found *one* other like me. So Hannah and Allie might not both be here. Or they might have found some other person who fell into the falls and got sucked across time by that matchmaking faerie. They might not be here at all—"

"Caroline." Callum placed firm, warm hands on her shoulders as she straightened her gown. "Dinnae forget to breathe."

She dragged in a ragged breath, but then she barreled on. "We can't waste any more time. If they aren't truly here…" She swallowed hard. "Then I want to know. And if they are here—one or both of them—"

"I ken," he said softly. "But even riding hard, it will take at least two days to cross the border and reach Saxford. And Bron and the others are waiting for me in the opposite direction."

When her mouth fell open in frustrated helplessness, he actually tossed his head back and laughed.

"I never kenned ye to be so impatient, my wee hellion." His dancing amber eyes captured her. "Ye will have to resign yerself to a few delays, but I truly believe we will find them. The woman said ye were one of the three women of the waterfall. The other two must be Hannah and Allie. And whether it takes a day or a sennight or a month—or more—I vow to help ye track them down."

"Thank you," she breathed, launching herself into his arms for a hard, swift embrace.

"Now," he said, setting her back from him. "We must ride to the nearby village to fetch Bron and the others. I cannae simply leave without alerting them, and besides, I dinnae plan on crossing into England without at least a few braw Highland warriors by my side. Then we will travel to Saxford as fast as ye can ride. Agreed?"

"Agreed." A thought occurred to her. "But what about—" Her gaze shifted through the trees beyond where Callum's horse stood, but to her bafflement, the multi-colored tent was no longer there. The wagon and mule were gone as well. "Where did she go?"

Callum followed her gaze, his brows winging in shock. "She must have some of the old ways in her, too," he murmured. "A witch—or mayhap only a seer, but touched by magic."

"But I don't understand everything she said. What if I can't find my sisters? What if—"

"She said ye could find all the answers ye sought," Callum said. "I believe we can—together."

Caroline gazed up at him, her heart swelling so large that it felt like it would burst from her chest. Hope filled her—for her sisters, for her future, for the destiny that had brought them all here.

Yes. Together.

Epilogue

"I dinnae ken," Callum said, for what felt like the thousandth time in the two days since they'd departed from Leannan Falls.

"Or what if it's Allie, and not Hannah?" Caroline continued, hardly seeming to hear his response. "Or neither of them. Do you think we could find that seer woman again if it turns out that whoever is at Saxford has nothing to do with my sisters?"

"I dinnae ken."

Bron shot Callum a droll look, but Callum only smiled. He would say it a thousand more times, for he didn't have the answers to Caroline's questions, but he loved that he got to hear her asking them.

She was here. She was staying. And if the wise woman's words proved accurate, her happiness could truly be complete—and then his would be, too.

Caroline shifted in his lap, a frown creasing her face. She'd forgone riding her own mare, just as she had on the last day of their journey to the falls, and Callum couldn't be happier. The feel of her warm, slim curves nestled against him was a constant reminder that she was real. And all his.

As if picking up the direction of his thoughts, she changed topics to her other favorite line of discussion on this trip. "I have an idea about our wedding."

"Oh?"

"I'd like to get married in the standing stone circle you showed me. That is, if the priest doesn't think that's too pagan."

Callum chuckled. "That I *can* answer. Father Padraig willnae take issue with a wedding in the stones—if it is the Laird's wish. As long as he is allowed to recite all the proper passages, he willnae cause a kerfuffle."

"Good. Because it is perfect. I can't wait to marry you there." She beamed at him, but then returned to gnawing on her lower lip in thought. "If my sisters really are in this time, do you think they would come to our wedding?"

Callum pursed his lips. "I dinnae ken." When her elbow connected with his ribs, he grunted. "But," he added, shooting her a mock glare, "I suppose it depends entirely on where they are. Travel isnae so easy, as ye've seen this last sennight, but it isnae impossible."

She nodded distractedly. "When that woman said the falls brought us together across time because we were soulmates, does that mean that if my sisters fell through with me, they also found soulmates? Or were they just along for the ride?"

"I dinnae—"

"Laird," Bron cut in, saving Callum from a response that would likely earn him another elbow to the ribs.

Bron pointed across the grassy, rolling landscape they rode through. Against the horizon, the North Sea was a ribbon of blue. A light breeze had carried the briny scent of the ocean to them all morning, but this was their first view of it.

Callum squinted against the sparkling water. A gray structure was perched in the distance at the point where land met sea.

"Saxford Castle."

Caroline tensed against him. There was no way she would be able to wait the hour or so it would take to ride at their current walking pace.

"Hold on," he murmured. When she looped her arms around him, he urged his horse into a gallop. His men followed suit, and the grass beneath their horses' hooves became a blur.

A hundred yards from the castle's wall, Callum reined in. He doubted the English lord who controlled this keep would take kindly to a band of Scottish warriors charging in at a gallop. He could see several guards eyeing them from the castle's gatehouses and battlements.

"Hold!" a faint English voice called from the wall. "Name yourselves and your business here."

"Bron," Callum said, jutting his chin from the warrior to the castle.

Bron nodded and kicked his horse into motion while the others waited behind.

Once he'd reined in below the castle walls, Bron's voice drifted to them on the wind.

"Laird MacMoran of Kinmuir Castle comes in peace," he began. "He wished to speak to the lord of the keep regarding the arrival of a particular lass who…"

In front of Callum, Caroline sucked in a hard breath. She began to tremble.

"What is it, love?"

"There." She lifted a shaky hand and pointed farther down the battlements, away from the guards. "That…that is…"

He followed her finger, his gaze landing on a woman standing in one of the crenellated openings along the stone wall. Her dark chestnut hair rustled softly in the salty breeze. Even from this distance, he could feel her ice-blue gaze landing on him and Caroline. The resemblance was unmistakable.

"*Hannah!*" Caroline breathed. "It's her. She really is here."

Her shoulders began to shake and the air left her lungs in a half-laugh, half-cry of joy.

"She's here," she mumbled through her happy tears. "Which means Allie might be here, too."

His chest swelled with happiness unlike aught he'd ever known. Caroline would have her family back. Her heart would be whole now, as would his, knowing she could stay with him without reservations or regrets. Only love.

She shook her head in wonder, her gaze fixed on her sister. "Hannah is afraid of heights. How the hell is she just standing there, so bold and confident?"

"I dinnae ken," Callum replied, a grin breaking over his face. "But we'd best go find out."

The End

CONTINUE READING the Enchanted Falls Trilogy with *Falling for the Knight* by Cecelia Mecca and *Falling for the Chieftain* by Keira Montclair!

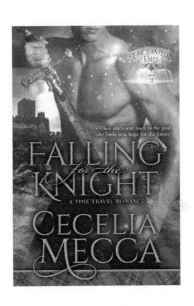

FALLING FOR THE KNIGHT
(ENCHANTED FALLS TRILOGY, BOOK 2)

BY CECELIA MECCA

When she's sent back to the past she finds new hope for the future.

Hannah Sutton prides herself on being a strong, independent woman, perfectly in control of her career and personal life. But her orderly existence is upended when she and her sisters travel to Scotland and jump off an enchanted waterfall as a lark. After blacking out, she finds herself marooned near a castle in England, alone. Everyone she meets appears to be a devoted reenactor, dressed from head to toe in medieval gear, but soon the truth becomes undeniable. Hannah has traveled back in time.

Tristan wasn't meant to be a lord, but his bravery and prowess in battle earned him the lordship of Saxford. Now, he faces a challenge that might very well unseat him—his ten-year truce with Saxford's biggest enemy is about to come to an end. It's the worst possible time for a mysterious woman to wash up on his beach, especially one who claims to be from the future. But the beguiling beauty quickly gets under his skin, and he realizes there might be something to her claim.

Hannah and Tristan have an immediate attraction that grows deeper, and the longer she stays at Saxford, the more she begins to question if she wants to return to the future—or make a future with her medieval knight.

Falling for the Chieftain
(Enchanted Falls Trilogy, Book 3)

by Keira Montclair

Fate reached across time to bring them together. Can love bridge their differences?

Allison Sutton isn't the sort to take risks. She's a nurse, so she's seen exactly where risk-taking can lead. But she leaves her comfort zone to visit Scotland with her sisters, and then takes a further leap of faith when one of them insists they jump from a waterfall that's supposedly enchanted. To her amazement, the jump brings her back in time, to the fourteenth century, and she comes face to face with a strapping Highlander who looks as if he's stepped out of her fantasies.

After his brother betrayed him, Brann MacKay has gone out of his way to display his prowess. Which makes it all the more embarrassing when he saves a slip of a lass from a crowd of men, only to earn a kick to the bollocks for his efforts. Even so, Brann is taken with the brash beauty. Allison is like no lass he's ever met, and he quickly realizes why. She emerged from the enchanted pool on his land. She wishes to return to her own world, but her knowledge of healing makes her indispensable to his people—and he quickly realizes she is indispensable to him.

Being with Brann makes Allison reconsider her stance on risks, but can a modern woman be happy with a medieval man?

Exclusive Offer

Make sure to sign up for my newsletter to hear about all my sales, giveaways, and new releases. Plus, get exclusive content like stories, excerpts, cover reveals, and more. Sign up at www.EmmaPrinceBooks.com

Thank You!

Thank you for taking the time to read *Falling for the Highlander*: A Time Travel Romance (Enchanted Falls Trilogy, Book 1)!

And thank you in advance for sharing your enjoyment of this book (or my other books) with fellow readers by leaving a review on Amazon. Long or short, detailed or to the point, I read all reviews and greatly appreciate you for writing one!

I love connecting with readers! Sign up for my newsletter and be the first to hear about my latest book news, flash sales, giveaways, and more—signing up is free and easy at www.EmmaPrinceBooks.com.

You also can join me on Twitter at @EmmaPrinceBooks. Or keep up on Facebook at https://www.facebook.com/EmmaPrinceBooks.

TEASERS FOR EMMA
PRINCE'S BOOKS

The Sinclair Brothers Trilogy:

Go back to where it all began—with Robert and Alwin's story in *Highlander's Ransom*, Book One of the Sinclair Brothers Trilogy. Available now on Amazon!

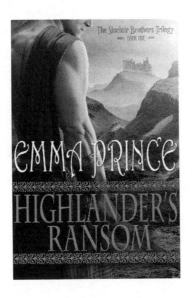

He was out for revenge...

Laird Robert Sinclair will stop at nothing to exact revenge on Lord Raef Warren, the English scoundrel who brought war to his doorstep and razed his lands and people. Leaving his clan in the Highlands to conduct covert attacks in the Borderlands, Robert lives to be a thorn in Warren's side. So when he finds a beautiful English lass on her way to marry Warren, he whisks her away to the Highlands with a plan to ransom her back to her dastardly fiancé.

She would not be controlled…

Lady Alwin Hewett had no idea when she left her father's manor to marry a man she'd never met that she would instead be kidnapped by a Highland rogue out for vengeance. But she refuses to be a pawn in any man's game. So when she learns that Robert has had them secretly wed, she will stop at nothing to regain her freedom. But her heart may have other plans…

Viking Lore Series:

Step into the lush, daring world of the Vikings with *Enthralled* (**Viking Lore, Book 1**)!

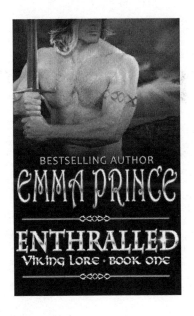

He is bound by honor...

Eirik is eager to plunder the treasures of the fabled lands to the west in order to secure the future of his village. The one thing he swears never to do is claim possession over another human being. But when he journeys across the North Sea to raid the holy houses of Northumbria, he encounters a dark-haired beauty, Laurel, who stirs him like no other. When his cruel cousin tries to take Laurel for himself, Eirik breaks his oath in an attempt to protect her. He claims her as his thrall. But can he claim her heart, or will Laurel fall prey to the devious schemes of his enemies?

She has the heart of a warrior...

Life as an orphan at Whitby Abbey hasn't been easy, but Laurel refuses to be bested by the backbreaking work and lecherous advances she must endure. When Viking raiders storm the abbey and take her captive, her strength may finally fail her—especially when she must face her fear of water at every turn. But under Eirik's gentle protection, she discovers a deeper bravery within herself—and a yearning for her golden-haired captor that she shouldn't harbor. Torn between securing her freedom or giving herself to her Viking master, will fate decide for her—and rip them apart forever?

Highland Bodyguards Series:

The Lady's Protector, the thrilling start to the Highland Bodyguards series, is available now on Amazon!

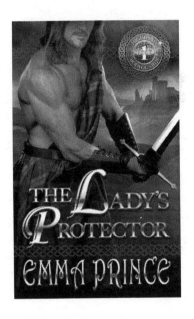

The Battle of Bannockburn may be over, but the war is far from won.

Her Protector...

Ansel Sutherland is charged with a mission from King Robert the Bruce to protect the illegitimate son of a powerful English Earl. Though Ansel bristles at aiding an Englishman, the nature of the war for Scottish independence is changing, and he is honor-bound to serve as a bodyguard. He arrives in England to fulfill his assignment, only to meet the beautiful but secretive Lady Isolda, who refuses to tell him where his ward is. When a mysterious attacker threatens Isolda's life, Ansel realizes he is the only thing standing between her and deadly peril.

His Lady...

Lady Isolda harbors dark secrets—secrets she refuses to reveal to the rugged Highland rogue who arrives at her castle demanding answers. But Ansel's dark eyes cut through all her defenses, threatening to undo her resolve. To protect her past, she cannot submit to the white-hot desire that burns between them. As the threat to her life spirals out of control, she has no choice but to trust Ansel to whisk her to safety deep in the heart of the Highlands...

About the Author

Emma Prince is the Bestselling and Amazon All-Star Author of steamy historical romances jam-packed with adventure, conflict, and of course love!

Emma grew up in drizzly Seattle, but traded her rain boots for sunglasses when she and her husband moved to the eastern slopes of the Sierra Nevada. Emma spent several years in academia, both as a graduate student and an instructor of college-level English and Humanities courses. She always savored her "fun books"—normally historical romances—on breaks or vacations. But as she began looking for the next chapter in her life, she wondered if perhaps her passion could turn into a career. Ever since then, she's been reading and writing books that celebrate happily ever afters!

Visit Emma's website, www.EmmaPrinceBooks.com, for updates on new books, future projects, her newsletter sign-up, book extras, and more!

You can follow Emma on Twitter at: @Emma-PrinceBooks.

Or join her on Facebook at: www.facebook.com/EmmaPrinceBooks.

27975813R00155

Made in the USA
Columbia, SC
03 October 2018